Petunia, for all the
Thanks for all the
good memories &
laughing
together!

Into the Desperate Country
a novel by Jeff Vande Zande

1/14/09

The mass of men lead lives of quiet desperation.
What is called resignation is confirmed desperation.
From the desperate city you go into the desperate country,
and have to console yourself with the bravery
of minks and muskrats. —Henry David Thoreau, *Walden*

Chapter I

Shivering, he stretched his legs into the blackness and tried to touch bottom. The river had narrowed, slowing the current, but the water was deeper. And colder. On either side the banks were black with tag alder. He was at least half a mile downstream, farther than he'd ever been. Could June still be waiting? She had to be all right. For a time he'd just floated, thinking about her, wondering if he'd made a mistake. Could she have been his chance at something closer to normal?

Still reaching, his toe touched the gravel bottom. Then he lost it again. Finding it seconds later, he tried to root himself. He was only able to keep light contact. The banks felt miles away. Ahead lay only more flowing blackness. He'd lost the feelings he had earlier, when he didn't care, when more than anything he had wanted to escape June and her question: "What will you do now?" He still heard her voice, but the question had more immediacy.

Minutes ago, he'd drifted with the current. He slowed when the river slowed and crawled over the bottom when it went shallow. Ignoring stumps, partially submerged logs, boulders just beneath the surface, shallow runs of rapid water, or any of the structures that Fish and Wildlife had put in, he'd moved thoughtlessly, easily, without fear. Drifting, he'd experienced the feelings he'd had at the cabin for the last three months. When he wanted to get out—as soon as he knew that he couldn't just drift—every possible way of harming himself rushed into his head. Skimming the bottom with his foot, he imagined jamming a toe against a log or rock. Maybe the hole would never shallow out. The river would get deeper—go into a reservoir. Thoughts like these seized him, and he began to thrash, going underwater a few times, surfacing to cough and spit out mouthfuls of water.

Despite his panic, the bottom rose to him. First he tiptoed, then walked on the balls of his feet, and finally moved normally up the slope and into water only three feet deep. The river widened and the tag alder thinned. He stopped moving, and the current worked around his legs.

He angled toward the knee-deep, then shin-deep water near shore. The pebble bottom gave way to mud. He sank past his ankles. The muck was colder than the water and it oozed up around his calves, musky and rotten, redolent of sewage.

He wrenched his feet out, imagining sharp branches that might be embedded in the soft bottom or the rare broken bottle. Everything on the water glowed in the moon's light. Downstream the river kept going without him, ghost-lit and gliding, until it finally turned a bend. Out of its pull, he saw it as beautiful again, something he wanted back. His breathing steadied. He stood and watched, and as he did June came into his mind. If he'd done this differently, he could be with her, naked in the cabin's darkness. It might have gone that far. There was no mistaking the signs. She'd wanted him.

Fire in the fireplace, romantic shadows. They would have made love. It had been a long time. She hadn't been asking him anything that anybody else wouldn't have asked. Her questions had been fair, even obvious. Why had he run away? His body shuddered violently. He turned from the water. Even with the moon, the river was bordered with much darker shadows. Where to go?

A tree lay in the water, its roots upended on the shore. As good a place as any to rest and figure out his next move.

"What are you going to do now?"

The surface spun in a slow eddy against the tree trunk. Nearby fish popped after bugs, and sometimes he heard the heavier slurp of a big brown trout feeding downstream. A constant breeze sidled through the treetops and chillingly around him. Part of him wanted to dive in again. Glowing in the moonlight, the river seemed his only path. It was, at least, going somewhere. His future seemed as dark as the black landscape of trees. He shrugged off the possibility of diving in again. Where did the river go? South. He knew that much. It passed under a road. He'd seen it on a map. What then? Hitchhiking would be impossible.

The tree was solid under his searching hand, bark rough. He sat on it, felt its coarse surface against his bare skin. He had no clothes. Naked. He shook his head. What had he been thinking? How had the day of fishing led to a night like this?

Chapter II

That afternoon, he'd felt the weight of the nightcrawler as it sailed through the air pulling line off his reel. For a moment the only thing he knew in the world was its brief flight. It was a good cast, just enough snap in his wrist to put the bait upstream from the dark pool, where it would tumble in naturally like any feed in the river. He pulled his arm back, stopping the cast short, leaving slack in the line so the worm would drift into the hole at the speed of the current. The heavy rush of water moved against his legs. In most places the river's pace was leisurely, but here, thirty yards below a rapids, the press was insistent, and he struggled to keep his balance. A wicker sound burst from his creel—the brown trout he'd caught earlier that afternoon thrashed, dying in the blackness.

His line pulled taut with the weight of the nightcrawler. He reeled in the bait. The large hole might be worth another cast. He'd learned that most holes on the Black, no matter what size, usually hit on the first cast, or they didn't hit at all. *No-brainer fishing*, his father called it. It lacked sport or any sense of finesse. As a young boy he had fished the Manistee with his father, and remembered picking up trout on the third or fourth cast into a hole, sometimes enticing a three or four pounder out of the safe shadows of a log. There was a mystery to that kind of fishing that he enjoyed. His father, a fly fisherman, always said that the fishing, not the fish, was the important part. He was only a boy then. At thirty-seven, he was beginning to understand what the old man meant.

Warmed by the memory of his father, he hit the spot one more time. He gave any fish that might be in the hole a moment to settle. The first cast and retrieve could have spooked them. The sun, too, had just come blazing out from behind a large cloud. In a minute or so, another sheet of clouds would swallow the light. He had a moment to look around him, a moment to breathe and think about nothing. Ahead were the river's riffles, pools, submerged rocks, and deadfalls. Along the banks the wind ruffled the long grass and rocked the black spruce and swamp hardwood rooted in stands a few yards from the river. On a nearby tree, a chickadee flitted from branch to branch. Its head jerked and twitched in a frenzied pivot. The silence in his mind was so complete that he could hear the slight fluttering of the bird's tiny wings.

A rustle. He turned in time to see the slick fur of an otter slip into the water. Its head emerged about fifty feet downstream then dropped into a pool around the base of a fallen jack pine.

He closed his eyes and imagined the otter's dive into the hole, sliding through the web of roots. Hugging the bottom, deep in the shadows, brown trout snapped their strong tails against the current.

He became the otter, moving quickly, hugging his claws into the spine and underbelly of a fish, biting it around the base of its head to stop its thrashing. He felt his jaw stretch around the fish's thick body. The joy of knowing hunger would soon end, the blood and bone happiness of satisfying the most basic of appetites. He dragged his prey into the wet grasses along the bank, flanked himself with the safety of some mud hole, and bit into the pinkish meat.

Seconds later, he opened his eyes. The sky was overcast. The otter surfaced again downstream. Its mouth was empty. It glided with the current until its head slipped under again. It didn't come up. He saw a fish rise and remembered why he was standing in the river.

He cast his bait upstream from the hole again. For a moment it tumbled with the current. Then his pole bent with the weight of something heavier than the sinkers and worm. Trout. He lifted the tip high, setting the hook, and let the fish make the next move.

"What are you going to do now?"

Its first effort was to swim hard across the river toward the deeper water of an undercut bank. Not a very big fish. It would soon be in his creel. With a potato and a hunk of bread, it would make a meal. Before long he was holding the writhing weight of a rainbow trout a little over ten inches long. Slipped into the dark creel, the fish began its mad thrashing. The other fish, dead or soon to be, did nothing. He looked downstream for a moment. He had enough fish. No place cool enough to keep a larger haul anyway. He could fish again the next day. Every day, if he wanted.

Sitting on a log, shivering naked in the middle of the night, he was jealous of the man he had been, the man who could think about fishing and nothing else. The cold river swirled around his legs. The day was still vivid in his head.

He buckled the creel and started the slow wade back to the bank, across the current. Most of the waterfront property was owned along this stretch. But nobody was here to accuse him of trespassing. He studied the knotty pine cottages and walked leisurely across the manicured grass. The owners probably working somewhere in Detroit or Pontiac or Flint. This weekend they'd be back, bringing the sounds of the suburbs with them, the laughter of children, barking dogs, the drone of lawnmowers. Sometimes, in the evening, the sound of canned television laughter drifted through his open window. He'd learned over the last couple months to stay near his cabin on the weekends, working in the garden or fixing things. He didn't want to see people. The disturbance would only be for a couple days. Late Sunday afternoon the cars fired up, fathers hollered for children and dogs, doors slammed, and gravel spit out from under tires. Everything became his again.

He didn't hate people, but talking to anyone might stop what he had started to discover—might take him off track. It wasn't good for a lot of people to see him anyway. People were probably looking.

A thick stand of trees grew on either side of the river just before his cabin. In the past he had tried to push his way through, but the heavy undergrowth slowed him. Hidden branches might puncture his waders. A long time ago someone had run a barbed wire fence through the trees, now rusted, impossible to step over in fishing gear. He'd often thought of taking it down or cutting a pass through it.

He eased his way back into the river and walked upstream. Within a few minutes he could see his property.

But something was different: a woman was watching him from the bank in front of his cabin. He stopped and blinked. She didn't disappear. She wore a blazer and business skirt. A briefcase rested against the front of her thighs. He studied her as he struggled against the current. She was thin, but not skinny. She had good curves. Even from twenty-five yards away she was pretty. She wore her blonde hair pulled up into a loose bun. Though he had imagined many times what this meeting might be like, he had never pictured that they would send a woman, especially not an attractive one.

"Mr. Carter?" she asked. She spoke loudly above the river.

"Yeah." It was the first word he had spoken in three weeks, and his voice sounded hoarse, older. Like his old man's. His heart thrashed like a fish in his creel.

She nodded. Then she watched him. The bank in front of his property was undercut and deep.

"Just give me a second," he said. He set his pole up near her feet. Finding purchase, he planted both palms on the bank to try to push himself up from the water. On his first attempt, his arms buckled and he sank back down. "Damn it," hissed from between his teeth.

The woman passed her briefcase into her left hand and took a step forward. "Can I help?"

"I got it." Her sweet perfume drifted down to him. He crouched as low as he could without getting water inside his waders. After a moment of breathing, he pushed and soon struggled his left leg onto the grass. With the added leverage he hoisted the other up and rolled over. She looked down and smiled at him. Early thirties he guessed. He'd been alone for a long time, but even discounting that, she was a knockout.

"Not usually someone here when I do that," he said, struggling to his feet. Her perfume was all around him.

"Maybe you could use a ladder or a rope?" She pushed a few strands of hair away from her eyes.

He looked at her and then at the bank. "Maybe. Wouldn't take much to build one." He looked back at her and then her briefcase. "Maybe not."

"I'm June Thorpe." She held out her right hand. "From Lenders One?"

He nodded and took her sweaty palm. "June's an unusual name nowadays. I like it."

She smiled and blushed slightly. "They just sent me out here…just to look at things. I'm just making sure there hasn't been any storm damage. I didn't think you'd be here. You are *Stanley Carter*, right?"

He guessed he should have told her no. He'd been sitting long enough that bugs were finding him, using his flesh as a landing zone. They didn't bite, and he didn't make any effort to brush them away. He half fell to sleep. Not so deep as to slide off the fallen tree. Every word of their conversation came back to him.

"Yeah. Well, Stan," he had said. About a month before, some high winds had whipped through the area knocking down trees. The storm kept him up all night. One cabin about a mile downstream lost part of its roof. He looked at her briefcase. He didn't want to hear what else she would say. "I got to clean these fish," he explained. She nodded. He knelt and unbuckled the leather strap on top of the creel. He took out the brown trout. It was dead, but not quite stiff yet.

"Why is there grass in there?"

He stuck the end of a filet knife down near the fish's anus and then slit it up to its gills. "Keeps the creel cool," he said. His fingers ripped out the guts. Then he dragged his fingernail down the black blood vein along the fish's spine. A moment later he started the other fish. He looked up at her once, thinking she'd be looking over his property, but she was watching him closely, especially his face. The gutted fish didn't seem to bother her. He liked that. Cleaning fish always bothered Rachel. June leaned towards him, and he tried not to glance down her top. It had been a long time. He tried to forget what her arrival meant.

"You're good at that," she said as he finished the second fish.

"Not much to it." With each thumb inside a fish, he closed the rest of his fingers around their spines and leaned over the bank to swish them clean in the water.

"The company has sent a lot of mail," she said behind him. "They left messages on your machine...until your phone was disconnected."

"I imagine," he said, back on his feet. "Let's go up on the porch so I can get these waders off." He stopped at the edge of the small garden he dug and tilled a few months ago. The green tops of vegetables poked out from the soil.

"Have you had anything out of there, yet?" she asked.

"Radishes."

"I love gardens," she sighed.

Nodding, he walked toward the porch again.

They passed his car. Leaves, pollen, dried rainwater, and dead insects had created a hazy, opaque film over it. He hadn't driven it since early July when the starter burned out. When he needed supplies, he walked to a gas station about two miles out on the main road. He mostly did without supplies.

Once up the porch steps, he shrugged off his suspenders and pushed down his waders. She was on the second step, watching him. "Sit down if you want." He motioned with his chin toward the rocking chair. Sunlight spread across the grass and the last of the clouds passed.

"I don't have everything here," she said. "I can't tell you everything. I didn't think I'd bump into you here." She stepped up onto the porch and sat in the chair.

He hung his waders on a peg and smiled. "Where do they think I am?"

"I haven't heard too many people talk about you, really. I talked to my boss a little bit before I came out, and he said you were probably dead, that they'd probably find you in some dumpster eventually. I'm really just out here to assess the property."

"Up here, people must think that everyone who lives around Detroit eventually winds up in a dumpster."

She smiled.

He sat down on the porch steps. "You saw me in the river?"

"Yes. I was looking around, and I could tell *someone* was living here. Then I heard you in the water." She looked at him. "I thought those things kept you dry."

His crotch and thighs were dark. "Sweat," he explained. When he looked at her, he was looking at places other than her green eyes. "I guessed someone would eventually come out to talk to me." He looked toward the river.

A moment passed. "Why are you here?"

He snickered. "We don't have to do this. Just open up the briefcase. I'll sign what I need to sign." His tone seemed to drain the color from her face.

She shook her head. "No, I really want to know. I don't have anything for you to sign," she said, her voice genuine and pleading.

He saw something in the way her eyes studied his face. She seemed to want to see something there, and when their eyes met, he had to turn away back toward the river. He reminded her of someone. Or maybe she found him attractive, too. Running his fingers into his curly beard, he remembered how long and shaggy his hair looked that morning in the mirror. If she was looking at him intently, it must have only been out of curiosity. "I guess I don't know why I'm here," he said.

"How long have you been here?"

"Three months."

"Are you okay?"

"I'm not out of my head. Don't think you have to soften me up. I know what I did. Just say what you have to say."

She was quiet before speaking. "You defaulted. The bank will foreclose and sell everything. This place, your house down in Farmington. That's what they do. I mean, they have to."

"I imagine." He looked back toward the river. "Can't really blame them." What more was there to say? Attractive or not, she represented the first step towards his losing everything.

"I still am curious to know though...I mean why you came here." Her voice was soft, almost ghostly.

He looked back at her, and they looked into each other's eyes. Hers looked tired. He didn't look away, and he felt his blood shifting. "Want a little whiskey?" he asked.

"No," she said. "Do you have anything weaker?"

"Whiskey and water."

She shrugged then nodded. "I'll take lots of water, though."

He went into the cabin to pour the drinks. He wondered where he would live after the foreclosure. How would he live? Everything was coming to an end. His tumbler was nearly half full. He swallowed it like a shot then refilled it. She was here, she seemed attracted to him, there was that. He imagined kissing her. Then Rachel slipped into his mind, and guilt.

Stepping out again, he handed her a drink that looked like the golden color the river became when it showed its sandy bed. His own was darker, more the color of the tea water that brewed in leafy puddles in the rain in the fall.

"This isn't bad...just a little sting," she said, after a cautious sip. She took a longer drink and coughed.

"You don't have to drink it," he said, chuckling.

"No, it's good." She took another sip. Then she slipped off her blazer. She looked at him and motioned towards the rocking chair.

He didn't say anything for a moment. "Oh, no, go ahead. I'm fine here." She had seen that he wasn't looking at her face. Flustered, he sat down on the steps. Her perfume filled the space of the porch.

"It's beautiful out here," she said. "My fiancé—well, my ex-fiancé—had a place like this on the Au Sable."

He nodded, looking out toward the water. Taking drinks, he tried to find a way to begin. Across the river a hornet's nest the size of a basketball dangled from a thin branch above the water. It seemed impossible, a defiance of gravity. Even from thirty yards

12

away he saw the insects swarming around the hole. He tried to imagine the buzzing hum in that hive, but couldn't. "I can't make any sense of it. Not in words."

"What did you do? Where did you work before this?" she asked.

He looked at her and smiled and then looked at her briefcase. "You don't already know? My life story's on that damn mortgage application."

"I didn't memorize it," she said. "I don't really know anything about you other than your residences. I drove over from Gaylord because the Detroit office asked someone from our office to check on the place. It's not like you're on my caseload."

He nodded. "I worked at an engine assembly plant in Novi."

"Did you hate it or something?" Her voice relaxed.

"Not like some guys do. I didn't really like it, but it paid good, I liked it for that. It bought me this place. Almost." He took another drink. "You see that? Fish jumped. Nice one, too."

She leaned out toward the water. She shook her head.

"Always loved this place," he said, his voice almost dreamy. "Came here every time I could talk them into it."

"Them?"

"My wife and daughter." He tilted his head and glass and finished his whiskey. He stood. "Lost them three years ago. Coming back from the dentist. Patch of black ice on I-696. Over the guardrail." He hated the way long rehearsal had telescoped it into a dozen or so words.

"Oh god, I'm so sorry." She looked as though she would stand.

Before she could, he said something about a refill, slipped through the screen door, and back into the dark cabin. Something hollowed his insides. It had been a long time since he'd mentioned their deaths. He'd thought about them, but talking out loud changed it. Standing at the kitchen counter, he breathed deeply until the urge to weep went away. When he came out, tumbler refilled, June had moved to the top step. "You can see the river better from here," she said. "I think I saw a fish jump."

If he hadn't been drinking, he'd have sat in the rocking chair, but the whiskey had him feeling good, and he knew that she was interested. His mind drifted to flesh. Thinking about her, imagining having sex with her, kept him from thinking of other things. He sat down next to her. She'd rolled her sleeves and pulled the bottom of her blouse out of her skirt. They both watched the river. Their hips were touching and she wasn't moving away. "Don't be so quiet. I can talk about it now."

"It's just so sad."

"Yeah, it was really sad. Probably part of the reason I'm here now. I mean, after the funeral I *did* go back to work. For three years I kept on the same way, as though they were still alive. I didn't really know anything else."

They grew quiet again. A cacophony of birds came in from the trees, like a symphony orchestra tuning up the instruments.

Stan stared across the river into the tree trunks that staggered back into the eventual darkness. How could he explain or even finish the thoughts he had started? "I wasn't thinking about them when I walked out of work that day," he began. "It was something that built up. On a Monday I looked down and I couldn't believe my hands were mine, like I was watching someone else's hands. I worked that way for three days, kinda outside of myself, and then I couldn't take it anymore and I walked. Just felt empty."

"I've felt like that," she said.

He nodded. "I had to get out, so I got in my car and drove here." He looked over at her. She finished her drink. He watched her lips on the rim of the glass. She coughed again when she pulled the glass away.

She cleared a tickle in her throat. "What will you do now?"

"Don't know. When I was a husband and father, I knew what to do. I kind of miss that…you know, knowing what to do. Even then, though, something wasn't quite right. I see that now. It wasn't them…my wife and daughter. I mean, I loved them. I still love them. It's more like something was missing sometimes in me, or I was missing something. I don't know. Now I'm just finding out each day what I need to do. And, whatever it is I'm doing, I like it…everything about it. Most of the time. Other times I feel like I'm nuts." He didn't mention the nights that their faces haunted him, the memories coming back. His crying would eventually settle into something like sleep.

"I know what you mean...about knowing what to do," she started. "When I was engaged, it just felt good like there was one big thing that I didn't have to worry about. I'd found someone. It made everything else easier. For a while." She looked down at the steps.

"I couldn't do it," June said a moment later, looking up. "I couldn't be out here by myself."

Stan took another sip and felt himself loosening. A dim haze of happiness tingled around him. He looked over at her. "Do you want another?"

She smiled. "No, thanks. I really have to get back to the office. I've already been gone too long."

"No," he protested. It was the first time in many months that he felt he needed to be with someone. "You have to stay." He smiled. "You have to explain everything that's going to happen...I mean with the bank."

"There's really nothing to explain..." she started, seriously.

"Well, just stay then...just for dinner. I want to eat dinner with someone." He smiled. "I'll cook those fish." He looked into her eyes and neither looked away.

"All right," she said, smiling.

Stan explained where the pantry was and said she should pick out whatever vegetable she wanted with the meal. She went into the cabin. When she came back, her arms were hugged around ears of corn. "I love corn. My mom used to stop at roadside stands all the time when I was a little girl," she explained excitedly. "She always seemed her happiest when she had a passenger seat full of sweet corn."

He made a fire in the pit. The electric company had long since turned off his power.

"You spend the night out here in the pitch black?"

"The dark's not scary."

In the fading light of the day, she fussed with the corn, pulling each stringy strand from between the kernels as she shucked. A breeze began to move the treetops. Stan set the filets in a frying pan with butter and pepper and worked them over a small alcove of hot coals. He looked around. The cabin. The river. The woods. He couldn't help but think about what was ending. Where would he go from here? Taking sips from his whiskey helped him to ignore his own questions.

"You have a pot for these?" she asked, holding the yellow out toward him.

"Inside. Above the sink."

She asked if he was okay.

"Fine." He forced a smile.

"This is fun," she said. "I feel like Laura Ingalls or something."

"It's great, isn't it?"

"It's nice for a change, a nice getaway." She stepped lightly up the stairs, across the porch, and into the cabin.

He watched her legs and felt content again as he listened to the sizzling fish.

After dinner they sat on the porch as dusk darkened towards night. Stan had apples in the pantry and suggested them for dessert. He tossed his core, and it splashed in the river. June rocked in the chair. He sat on the top step. Each time he looked back more of the details of her face were faded into silhouette.

"What *are* you going to do now?"

She'd asked the question he'd been trying not to ask himself ever since she'd shown up. "Don't know," he said.

She asked if he could go back to the plant.

"No. And I wouldn't want to." He stood, went back into the cabin, and poured himself another whiskey.

Plans. He didn't have any.

He listened for the churn of the river.

"Would you think of working up here somewhere?" she asked. "My brother manages a couple movie theaters. Maybe he could get you a job."

"Really don't know. Haven't thought about work that much." He took a long drink. He would need money eventually. "Have you ever swum at night?" he asked.

"No!"

"I do it every night. The river's cold, but there's a hole right in front of the cabin here where the current slows down a bit." The idea of swimming with someone excited him.

"I'm not swimming in the dark. I don't even have a swim suit," she said.

"Well, all right, just come down to the river and watch me then."

She looked at him. "Can't we just stay up here? It's getting cool. Couldn't you make a fire in the fireplace?"

He wished he could go back to that moment. His legs were numb. For some time, the moon was obscured by clouds. The darkness was thicker around him. He shifted on the bark. He could change everything if he could get back to that moment. He could make a fire. He could be with her.

"Afterward I'll make a fire," he had said. "I won't swim for long."

She followed him off the porch. "I can't even see where I'm going."

He turned around, took her hand, and led her down to the water. As they walked, their fingers moved and then twined together, just before he let go.

The river was moving blackness. Its murmur was louder than it was during the day. A reflection of the moon wavered in the slower water on the other side.

"I can't believe you're going to swim in there."

"Well, I am." He began to strip down.

"God, you could give me some warning," she said, turning.

He laughed and apologized. "Sorry, I'm still getting used to the idea of other people." He set his clothes in a pile and then jumped out from the bank into the water. He yelped at the cold. Then, setting his feet down, he rooted himself into the river bottom and was able to stand.

"It's so buggy."

Her silhouette sat on the bank. He was glad. A light snow of insects played on the surface of the water. "I think they're white mayflies or something. They don't bite, not like mosquitoes."

"Something is biting." She slapped her neck.

He let his legs drift up and crawled against the current. After a time, he'd made no progress upstream but hadn't been pushed downstream either. He was breathing hard when he stopped. He could see a little now. She'd removed her shoes and her feet dangled in the water. Her hands were busy brushing bugs from her face and slapping them from her arms and neck.

"I could help you, you know," she said. "With the bank."

"What?" he asked. Why couldn't she just let it go?

"You don't have to lose everything. There are people I can talk to. Banks don't want to foreclose. Better for them if everyone goes on paying their interest. You don't really want to lose your house."

And to keep from doing that, he knew what he'd have to do. To hold onto his house and pay the property taxes, he'd need to work in the strictest sense. The kind of work that they pay you for, and the only reason that you do it is because they pay you. The kind of work that you contort your hands and mind into to make them fit. It seemed ugly to him, selling your life by the hour. Nothing was worth it.

"You wouldn't want to lose this place, would you? You're going to have to do something." She spoke just loud enough to be heard above the river. Just above a whisper, but he heard it as if her lips were next to his ear.

The cold water started to numb his body. He needed to keep moving. No glow left from the whiskey. She was saying what he'd refused to let the voice in his head say. She was asking the questions he didn't want to answer. He couldn't blame her for asking. If he left, he knew he'd never get back to the place he had achieved in the last three months. If he tried to stay, the bank would foreclose and he'd be removed from the property forcibly. Either way, he would lose everything. Again. He shivered, not only from the cold water, but from something bigger than cold. He was cornered.

"Stan?" she asked.

No, he thought. No. He turned, dove, and swam underwater with the current. He knew the river here. There was nothing for him to run into. He became the otter again, moving smoothly with the dark water. His lungs burned. He stayed under for as long as he could. When he surfaced he was far downstream. The moon glowed brightly. Thousands of insects flew around his head—nymphs unfolding at the surface into wings. He wasn't sure if June could see him, or if his head just looked like flotsam, but she screamed his name. He didn't answer, and the current swept him out of the luminescence and into the blackness of a bend in the river.

Chapter III

Stan wondered what June did afterward. He looked up at the moon, which had slid far to the west. He must have slept for a few minutes on the log downstream from his cabin. How long did she wait? She didn't like being alone in the darkness. He ached with guilt as he pictured her stumbling back from the river trying to find her car.

Something loosened from a tree above him, and the stoop of a predator bird whooshed over his head. He ducked. A moment later a small animal squealed its death in the brush. Then it was silent again, except for the river and the wind. He became aware of a droning in the woods. It was so low pitched he hadn't noticed it before. Or maybe it was what woke him up. It wasn't natural. Sounded like idling engine, refrigerator, air conditioner. He turned towards it. Lights—a cabin. In a warming rush of relief, he picked his way to shore. He pushed through a thin wall of tag alder and small cedars and felt lawn under his feet. He was thankful for the soft grass. The outline of a small cabin appeared in his adjusting eyesight. A silhouette moved past one of the windows.

He remembered he was naked. He couldn't just knock on the door like some kind of lost streaker. He rubbed his arms vigorously. He couldn't get warm. He crept closer to the cabin looking for anything that he might cover himself with—a forgotten towel, a t-shirt, a pair of fishing waders, tarp. Nothing.

Within feet of the cabin, he distinguished the rise and fall of jazz coming from within.

"Goddammit!" a man's voice exploded from inside.

Stan waited for nearly a minute. What the hell was that yelling about? The jazz stopped, and the deep voice of a DJ began. The man inside the cabin didn't speak again. Something rustled in a nearby stand of trees. Stan listened. Crouching in the dim glow from the windows made everything beyond the cabin's perimeter seem darker. His testicles tightened beneath him. If the man had been yelling at someone, another person hadn't responded.

Small silhouettes flitted across the moonlit surface of the river. Bats. After the white mayflies. He and his friends used to wait for the bats to come out in their neighborhood. Using wrist rockets or slingshots, they fired balled-up pieces of aluminum foil into their flight paths and laughed as the bats attacked the foil balls.

Kids.

It was stupid, but it was the kind of thing that would entertain a certain level of boredom. They tormented the bats for hours. Stan's friends were all older than him. He had always hung with an older crowd. In sixth grade, he smoked cigarettes with eighth graders. In ninth grade, he hung around with the juniors who had cars. He drank and smoked pot. When he was a senior, most of his friends worked in the auto plants and had apartments. He partied with them and prayed that school would soon end. The summer he graduated, he stood in three of his friends' weddings. He had always been in a hurry to follow their lead.

A light went out in the cabin, leaving only one window lit. His pulse raced at the thought of those inside going to sleep. He had to try something. If he knocked on the door, they would open it to a naked man. Not the way he wanted to start things.

"Hello?" he called. "I'm out here. I need help."

He waited. Nothing changed in the cabin. The DJ's voice segued into more jazz. Another violent shiver rattled his body. When had the nights started to get so cold? He imagined June was in her car on her way home. Was she worried? Did she call the police? Would there be search parties? "Hello?" he shouted above the wind. "Hello. I'm outside your cabin, and I think I need some help."

The jazz died.

Despite the cold, he suddenly felt hot. He knew it had started. His new life. Outside a stranger's cabin in the woods of northern Michigan. Without clothes. He wanted to run, dive into the river, keep going. He couldn't. He would have to try to figure out his next move, the image of which eluded him. "What are you going to do now?"

No more lights came on in the cabin, but someone was moving.

The night screeched with the familiar friction of a sliding glass patio door. Up close to the cabin, Stan couldn't see the door or who was standing in its frame. On the ground in a rectangle of dim light, a man's shadow appeared. Stan cleared his throat.

"Someone out here?" the man asked gruffly.

Stan was silent for what seemed like too long. He couldn't find his voice. "Yes," he managed weakly.

The pump of a shotgun ratcheted. "Did you hear that?" the man asked.

Adrenaline burned in Stan's stomach and left a tinny taste in his mouth. He stood and stepped back, wanting at least to see who was talking to him.

"You better stop moving around," the man warned.

"Look, I'm lost. I was on the river, and I didn't know where I was, and then I saw the lights on here."

"Are you hurt or something?"

"Just freezing. And..." As soon as they left his lips, he doubted whether these were the right words. His body shook.

"Well, you're not far from the Carson Road access. Are you in a canoe or wading?"

"I was swimming."

"Swimming!"

"Swimming."

"Come over here where I can see you."

Stan took a few steps towards the voice. The silhouette of both the man and the gun were framed in the doorway. The barrel pointed toward the ground.

"Can you see me?" Stan asked. He heard the childlike pitch in his voice, the innocence he was trying to create, and he hoped the man heard it too. Could he see that Stan was naked?

"Yeah, I see you," the man said. "So what happened? Did you roll your canoe or something?"

"It's a long story, really," Stan started. "I've been out of the water for a while and I'm pretty cold." The idea of telling the story, the real story, exhausted him. He hoped he wouldn't have to, not standing naked like this. What a fool.

"You probably need to come in, need to call someone or something?" The man's voice grew kinder.

Chapter IV

Two lamps dimly lit the inside of the cabin. Towel wrapped around him, Stan waited on an outdated plaid couch that smelled faintly of empty rooms. Dale had gone into another room, somewhat flustered, to find him clothes. Dale's cabin had many of the amenities that Stan had seen in other cabins: a large-screen television, a fine stereo, all of the appliances of a fully stocked kitchen, including a dishwasher. His own cabin had none of these things, besides an old forties radio that picked up one or two static-muffled stations. It was one of the reasons Rachel stopped wanting to go to the cabin.

"Does it have to be so rustic? It's my vacation too. All you do is fish—I have to cook and clean all weekend. Does it have to be so uncomfortable?"

He had never felt anything but comfortable there, maybe the only place where he truly felt comfortable. And he would soon lose it. The room seemed darker.

"I don't know if these will fit you," Dale said, stepping through a door just off of the kitchen. He held a pair of jeans and a sweatshirt. "You're a little shorter than me, but we might have around the same waist. You a thirty-six?" He wouldn't look at Stan.

"Thirty-eight." Dale was in his late fifties or early sixties. His hair was gray, but thick. His eyebrows, thick black, looked like wooly bear caterpillars before a hard winter.

"Well, try them anyway. Bathroom's over there." Dale motioned with his chin towards another door.

Stan went into the bathroom. The pants pulled on easily. He'd lost quite a bit of weight while living at the cabin. He folded the pant legs into a cuff until his feet were clear. He corkscrewed the sweatshirt down over his head and looked in the mirror. Bold black letters on the front of the sweatshirt read "**OLD FISHING FART.**" He grinned. Dale was all right.

"You want something to drink?" Dale called.

"I'll take whiskey if you have it." He started to dry his hair with the towel and thought of June again. She had wanted a fire in the fireplace. She wanted to sit with him in a cabin with no electricity. He smirked. Instead he'd be sharing a fire with Dale.

"Scotch okay? I'll pour you a Glenfiditch," Dale said. "How does everything fit?"

"The pants are a little long, but good in the waist. Thanks a lot. I really appreciate this." Stan's own face surprised him in the mirror. It'd been a long time since he'd seen himself in such bright light. Long hair. Thick beard. Grizzly Adams. Well, Grizzly, anyway. He could only imagine what Dale was thinking.

"Don't mention it," Dale returned. "Maybe I'll put a sign down by the river: 'Skinny Dippers' Refuge.'"

"Yeah," Stan said, eased by Dale's humor, something that the shotgun didn't suggest earlier. He found a razor and cut away some of the more scraggily hair high on his cheeks. He stopped and stared into his own eyes. Something happened and his head lightened. He looked around. Nothing helped him feel any more grounded. Dark, knotty pine walls, the soap dispenser with the ceramic rose, the antique mirror. Familiar as his own fingerprints, yet none of it was familiar.

"Stan?"

"Yeah?" he returned, shaken.

"I asked if you take anything with your whiskey."

"Just straight is fine." Stan opened the bathroom door. Anything in Glenfiditch would be an insult.

He stopped in front of the fireplace. The smoldering embers of a fire hissed quietly. He could have shared a fire with June tonight if he hadn't been so stupid, so jumpy. Maybe he could have shared more. The only woman he'd been with for years was his wife.

"You okay?" Dale asked. He handed Stan a tumbler of whiskey.

"Yeah. Cold water just gave me a headache." He tried to imagine what was next. The idea of working on the line again left him feeling heavy and drugged. But what otherwise? A new job? He sipped the strong whiskey. Was there still time to sell his house, pay the bank back, and even make a small profit? That would buy him some time to figure out his next move. He stared into the embers.

"What are you going to do now?"

After he'd lost Rachel and Shannon, his sister tried to get him to see a therapist. He refused. Maybe it would have been a good idea. Had he dealt with the loss right? A good shrink might have been able to help.

"The clothes look good, really," Dale said. He cleared his throat. "I'm sorry about the sweatshirt." He pointed at the words. "It's the only warm shirt I had around here. My kids bought it for me a few birthdays ago."

"It's fine. Great, in fact. Fits me perfectly. Thanks again." He took a sip of his whiskey, much better than the stuff he had at his cabin. Fragrant of smoke and peat. Top shelf.

Dale eased into a recliner. He seemed to move cautiously, as though there were a sick person in the room that he might wake. "Phone's over on the counter if you need to call someone."

Stan went back to his place on the couch. He wanted to see the river, but the darkness pressed up against the sliding glass door made it a mirror. In the dark reflection Dale studied him. Brow furrowed, his look was a mix of apprehension and concern.

He asked again if Stan was okay.

Stan nodded. "Just tired." He leaned back into the couch.

"Use the phone whenever you want. I'll be right back." Dale stood and walked into the bathroom. He peeked out again. "Phone's on the counter."

Who could he call? His parents were dead. His wife and daughter were gone. His sister? For months after his loss she called every weekend from California, tried to get him to talk, but he'd insisted that there wasn't anything to talk about. "Jesus Christ, Debbie, what the hell do you want from me?" After a time he just stopped answering the phone.

Dale ran water in the bathroom. Stan felt weighed down. During the months at his own cabin he'd felt the cares of the world falling away, one by one. Weightless. Nothing seemed right to him in Dale's cabin, not the strange furniture, the strange clothes, the strange whiskey. He felt like he'd stumbled into someone else's dream. Strange or not, he drank the scotch, hoped it would lift him into a mood that Dale would be able to tolerate. He was probably wondering what he had let into his cabin.

He thought of June. She was like a prayer in his mind, a vision. If he was going to start over, she'd be a good start.

"Jesus Christ," Dale hissed from the bathroom. He flushed the toilet.

Stan looked around the dim room. Something popped in the embers. His mouth and cheeks tingled from the whiskey. He welcomed it. It was good to feel something other than the weight of his thoughts. He took another long drink and emptied his glass. June. She wouldn't leave his mind. She was a whisper of something better. Something solid.

But she made him jumpy, anxious. If she could have just dropped the questions. "Yes," he whispered to himself. The idea of going back to his cabin—the solitude—seemed suffocating. A night alone in the darkness with nothing to do but think. What would that amount to? He marched into the kitchen and absently poured himself another whiskey. Then, looking at the bathroom door, he sat down on the couch again. Maybe Dale didn't want some stranger drinking up his best booze.

Dale stepped back into the room. He looked agitated. "Did you call anybody?" he asked, sitting in the recliner again.

"Nobody to call, really."

Dale took a drink. "Are you sure you're okay because I don't—" he started, drumming his palms against the arm of the chair.

"I'm fine. I just don't have anyone to call. But I don't really need anyone. My cabin's upstream from here. I just need to get out to M-74 and then I can walk back to my place." But then what? He wouldn't sleep. And, in the morning—what then? Hitchhike into Gaylord?

Remembering his useless car, Stan ran his fingers through his hair. "I guess I just need to borrow these clothes. I can get them back to you sometime in the next couple days." Maybe he could get his car's starter to work one last time. He remembered a neighbor who used to crawl under his car and whack his starter with a pipe wrench at five every morning. Did he have a pipe wrench?

A clock chimed ten times.

"No hurry on returning the clothes," Dale assured him. "And, I can take you out to 74. I have to go out." He turned the right side of his head towards Stan. "You like that? You haven't said anything about my earring."

He squinted towards Dale. At first whatever was in the lobe was a blur, but he soon realized that it was a dry fly, the hook all the way through, and a few inches of tippet dangling from the eye.

Dale turned back to him. "Nice, huh? About thirty minutes before you showed up, I was out on the river trying to pick up a brown. Wind caught my cast just right and I put the hook through my ear." Dale shook his head. "You fly fish?"

"My dad did."

Dale nodded. "I've been trying to get the damn thing out, but I just can't pinch the barb right." He held his hand as though he were holding a pair of pliers. "I was getting ready to drive to the hospital when I heard you outside. I guess I can still go. Emergency room should be pretty slow this time of night." He set his empty glass in the sink. "Even if I got it out, I'd need a tetanus shot."

Stan finished his glass in one swallow. "Are you going into Gaylord?" He imagined seeing June that night. She was his chance. He had to do this while he had the fire in his belly. In the morning, after a night of staring into the dark ceiling of his cabin, he might not be brave enough anymore.

"Yeah," Dale said. "I gotta go in. I can't sleep with this thing in my ear."

Something mixed with the booze and rushed through Stan's blood. "Could I ride with you?" he asked, guessing that June would have to be in the phone book.

Pulling a windbreaker from a coat hook, Dale turned a puzzled look toward Stan.

"Actually," Stan explained, "I have a friend in Gaylord."

"It'll be almost eleven by the time we get there."

"I'm hoping she'll be up." Stan smiled.

"She." Dale smiled, too. "All right," he said, "But you won't need a ride back, will you? Because I don't know—"

He shook his head reassuringly. "No. No. I'll be all set. I'll just get out at the hospital and walk from there. It's close by," he lied. He was certain this would be the start to his new life or at least the start to something. Or the end of something. What are you going to do now? He looked at the clock. "Is it really after ten?"

"No," Dale said. "I keep that clock about a half hour fast. It's a little trick I use to keep myself on time."

"Does it work?"

"Nope."

Chapter V

S tan pulled his door shut. Stale cigar smoke wafted from the seats. Dale slid in behind the steering wheel and turned on the lights.

"Jesus Christ, the wind," Dale said. "Are we going to Gaylord or to Oz."

Stan sniffed a laugh.

"Look at that." Dale pointed at the windshield.

At least a thousand white insects crawled over the outside of the glass. They jittered about in an orgiastic frenzy.

"I saw them earlier on the river," Stan said. "They're white mayflies or something, aren't they?"

"Ephorons," Dale corrected. "It's underrated, but sometimes I catch more fish during an ephoron hatch than I do during the Hex hatch." He studied them for a few seconds and then turned on his wipers. "Sorry guys." The blades swept them aside like so much fallen snow.

"My dad said they only have wings for a couple days," Stan said. Insects collected on the glass again.

Dale nodded. "They're nymphs most of their lives…under water sometimes for years. It's amazing they even know what to do with wings when they finally hit the surface. Then it's sex and death."

Stan watched the insects. "It's funny," he said. "Just given wings like that…you'd think they'd want to fly more, at least for a little while."

"It's not like they think about it," Dale said.

The two-track slithered under them as Dale maneuvered the Cadillac behind the headlights. It looked like every other dirt road Stan had driven in the dark. Washouts, ruts, long-standing mud puddles, stretches of sugar sand, and all of it served to slow Dale to a crawl. Stan fidgeted in his seat. June would be asleep if they didn't speed up. Trees flashed briefly into the headlight and as quickly disappeared. It wasn't long before they turned onto a groomed road. But Dale didn't speed up. Stan fought the urge to tell him to hurry.

"Even on a road like this you can kick up a rock and knock something loose on your underside," Dale said, as though sensing Stan's impatience. His hands moved on the steering wheel.

Stan glanced at the speedometer. Fifteen miles an hour. They'd have to hit blacktop soon. June, her soft hair, generous body, haunting green eyes. He heard her voice. She was what he needed. It made sense. Outside his window the blackness seemed motionless.

Dale hit the brakes. Stan lurched forward until the seatbelt caught him. "Look," Dale said. His pointing finger directed Stan's attention off to the right.

He looked into the blackness. "I can't see anything. What am I supposed to be looking at?"

Dale shifted and the car started to roll backwards.

Stan clenched and then released his fists.

"See them now?" Dale asked. His voice was excited, risen.

Exhaling, Stan looked again. Nothing. He sighed. Then, they appeared. More than twenty small orbs glowed at him from where there had been only darkness a moment ago. Eyes. He'd seen deer at night before, but never so many together at one time. His anxiousness ebbed for a moment. He started to count.

"You see them, right?" Dale asked. "That's why I never fly down these roads. Most people think that they're only around at dusk, but I've come across big herds like this as late as two in the morning. If you're not careful, you can put one through the windshield pretty easily." He shifted into park.

Stan nodded. The eyes didn't move. Behind them the faint outlines of the deer began to appear. Many of their heads were cocked towards the car, but a few had gone back to grazing. Dale pulled the shifter into drive. Stan almost asked him to wait. He'd had moments like these at the cabin, awed by something simple and untamed, like wild turkey cutting through in the morning or a crayfish claw on the river bottom. The car rolled forward.

Past the herd, Stan stared into the darkness. He was puzzled by a sudden urge. He wanted to ask Dale to stop so he could get out and walk into the tangled woods. How many other animals were within five hundred feet of the car in the darkness, not needing the road or the light, not needing anything other than instinct? A distant point shone out of the night. He turned his head, tried to keep the light, but it disappeared. He guessed it was a cabin.

"Who's the girl you're going to see?" Dale asked. "Maybe she has an older sister who likes guys with earrings."

Stan laughed. An urge to talk, to confess, rose to his surface.

"Okay, I want to tell you everything." He started with the deaths of Rachel and Shannon, why he went to the cabin, why June came by, and why he ended up naked on Dale's property. Miles passed. Wind rocked the car in gusts as Stan spoke.

Dale pulled up to the pumps at a gas station a moment after Stan stopped talking. There were no other buildings around. He turned the engine off. He didn't open his door right away. Stan stared out the windshield at the haze of insects around the lights overhead. His story was probably more than the poor guy wanted to know. Still, it felt better to tell someone. The odor of gasoline leaked into the car.

"I'm really sorry about your wife and daughter," Dale said. He reached over and squeezed Stan's shoulder.

"It's okay," he said. "I'm okay."

Dale got out. Soon the silence thumped heavily to the rhythm of the pumping gas. As a little girl, Shannon had always begged to help Stan at the pumps. He had enjoyed being a father.

Dale tapped on the window. "You want anything from inside?" he asked, motioning towards the store.

Shaken from his memories, Stan was glad to leave them behind. For the first year after losing them, he'd fall into long, numbed trances several times a day. Convinced that this was unhealthy he tried, as much as he could, to not think about them.

He opened his door. The night felt warmer. Bags of corn leaned against the pumps. Could deer season be that close already? Beyond the fluorescent halo around the gas station, everything else was black. "I'll come in with you and look around," he said.

They started across the parking lot. Stan picked his way slowly, stopping to brush pebbles from his soles.

"You don't even have shoes," Dale said.

Stan looked down. Dale shook his head. "I should have given you an old pair of mine. What the hell was I thinking?"

"It's okay. I'll manage."

Dale asked again if Stan wanted anything. "Are you hungry?"

He didn't seem in a hurry, despite his ear. The older man, having heard his story, was probably treating him gingerly. A new urge came to Stan that he hadn't felt in a long time. He suddenly wanted a cigarette. He hadn't smoked since his early twenties. The idea of lighting, drawing in the smoke, exhaling struck him as something that might settle his jumpiness. Saliva seeped into his mouth. At one point he was smoking a pack a day.

"What brand?" Dale asked.

"I don't know."

"You don't know?"

"Anything's fine. Something cheap, I guess. Lights, though." He felt stupid and wished he hadn't asked. "You don't have to buy them. I shouldn't have asked."

Dale studied him for a second. "I don't mind."

Above them, the blizzard of insects bounced frantically off the lights.

Chapter VI

They took a back way into Gaylord. They never got to I-75 as he thought they would. For miles everything appeared to be the same. In front of him, the unchanging orange and green lights of the dashboard. From the corner of his eye, he was aware of the small, constant movements of Dale's hands on the wheel. And, beyond that, past the black of the hood, the road came out of the darkness into the high beams. It curved slightly at times and, at the edges, the gray trunks of trees flickered by, but it all felt the same. The blacktop hummed endlessly beneath them.

Cold settled into his feet. The matted flooring was damp and pimpled with pebbles. He searched for a dry spot. His situation became clear to him. He was driving into Gaylord to see a girl who probably hated him, or at the very least thought he was crazy. He didn't know where she lived. He had no wallet, no shoes, and someone else's clothes. Why hadn't he asked Dale to drive him back to his own cabin? He could have at least changed and picked up his wallet. He turned the pack of cigarettes over and over.

"You can smoke," Dale said, breaking the silence.

"What?"

"In the car, I mean. I have a cigar in here sometimes." He pushed the cigarette lighter into the dash. "Go ahead."

Stan smacked the pack against his hand. He worked a cigarette out and touched the orange coils of the lighter against it. He took a drag and held the smoke in his cheeks. Then he exhaled. He remembered his very first time and how he'd been afraid to inhale. His friends teased him until he did, throwing himself into a coughing fit.

The passenger side window slid down, and the smoke that was pooling in front of him turned snakelike and slithered out into the darkness. He looked over at Dale who was looking at him. "Sorry," Stan said.

Dale smiled. "Don't worry about it." He moved his finger from the automatic window switch.

Stan took another drag and sucked some of it into his lungs. He coughed it back out. Without looking at Dale, he took another drag and was able to hold it and exhale it a little more smoothly. The nicotine rushed through him. He sunk a little more comfortably into his seat. A good feeling swirled into his head. His cheeks tingled.

"Can I say something to you?" Dale asked.

"Sure." He didn't know what to expect.

"You made it pretty clear that you don't know what's next for you," Dale started, "and I think that's okay. You'll find your way in that respect—some kind of job will come along. That's not the tough part, really. I guess anyone who really wants to work can find work." His hands left the steering wheel for small gestures.

Stan hadn't said anything about wanting to work.

"But, I agree with you about this girl. I mean, I don't know if I'd have the nerve to show up at her place this late. And, maybe that's not the best way to go, but you seem to think you'll make it work."

Stan stared ahead and watched the darkness release the oncoming road into the headlight. Where was Dale taking the conversation?

"What I'm saying is that I think you're on the right track by trying to start something with her. These feelings, the idea that what you need is to find somebody. That's what's going to really make the difference. I just think that's what it's about anymore." His right hand chopped the air.

Stan wasn't sure what to say. Having only smoked half of it, he flicked his cigarette out the window. He found the button and watched the glass slide back up.

"When I think over what I know now, I wouldn't have let my divorce happen so easily." Dale sat quietly.

"When did it happen?"

"Fifteen years ago. I think about it more now than I ever did then. Then, it just seemed like something that happened to everybody. Most of my friends were divorced. Our kids were out of the house. She said she wanted a divorce, and it seems like I just shrugged and said, 'Okay.' I'm sure I did more than shrug. Maybe I asked why, but what I remember asking was if there was another man. I tried to turn it around to place blame on her, explain things that way. But, there was no other man. It was just me. It was nearly seven years before she remarried. She went back to school first."

"Back to school?"

"She went back and became a nurse. Then she met another nurse."

"Oh," Stan said. "Then it was—"

"No," Dale said, chuckling. "Got you, though. No, she met a guy nurse. An older guy, too. They have a place in Brighton. The kids say she's still really happy. I guess I'm happy for her, but I miss her too. Isn't that funny?" He shrugged his hands open and then took the wheel again. "Fifteen years ago already."

The road kept coming at them and it, like Dale's words, seemed to be going somewhere, slowly. "Do you have any idea...I mean, do you think you know why it really happened?" He thought of his own marriage. He and Rachel had been close to splitting up a few times. They'd never said as much, but he'd felt it.

"I guess now I know why it happened...or at least I think I know," Dale continued. "After the kids were gone, she had time to look around, and I don't think she liked what she saw. She worked when we were first married. She helped out in a first grade class—not volunteer or anything. This was paid. And, she liked it. But when she got pregnant, I guess it seemed silly for her to keep that job when I was working. Lawyer. We'd done everything right...waited until I was making good money before we tried for kids. At the time, I think she gave the job up pretty easily. But after, after the kids were in college, she felt restless again. She talked about going back to school. It made me mad at the time. Here the kids were out of the house, and we could do whatever we wanted you know, vacations and things, and she wanted to get tied down to a college schedule." Dale exhaled. "I was selfish and didn't support her at all. I'd yell so much sometimes that I'd get her crying. So, I mean, I think it was *me* because I couldn't really see what I needed to see. And now, I'm getting close to retirement, and I come up here a lot by myself. I try to get the kids to come up and bring their kids, but it's tough. They're out of state. So, I'm alone a lot."

Stan rubbed his hands together. He had no clear reason why his own marriage had seemed at times like it was falling apart. They would go into a dark place. They'd be like two strangers who'd agreed to keep a house together, pay the bills, build for the future, smile when the little girl who lived with them was around. Sometimes they could barely stand to be in the same room. And this could go on for weeks. It was as though they'd run out of words. Run out of passion. All the overtime he worked didn't help, but they needed the overtime so they could do things they wanted to do. It was during these times that he'd wait for her to say she wanted a divorce. She just seemed so sad, so unhappy. But, for no clear reason, the funks would end, and they'd speak to each other again, make each other laugh, make love. They'd been in one of their down times when Rachel died.

"It's not as bad as all that," Dale said. "I'm not some love-struck teenager contemplating suicide. It's just sometimes I think about what I had. I miss it. But maybe I just think it would be good. Who knows, maybe we wouldn't talk to each other at all if we were still together. When the idea of marriage started, people didn't live much past thirty-five. It was easy to stay together." He shrugged both hands into the air, palms up.

"Rachel and I had our rough patches," Stan said, feeling melancholy. "We were only together for thirteen years. If it had been longer, who knows. Maybe we—"

"Goddammit," Dale sighed, "I'm sorry. I didn't want things to go like this. I started out...but then I got into my marriage and things... What I meant to say is that this is all we have—being with someone else." He reached for the radio and then drew his hand back.

"I don't think I'm making any sense," Dale said.

"No, I'm following you," Stan said. He felt the familiar heaviness weighing on him again.

"How can you be?" Dale asked. "I sound like some depressing old guy with a lot of regrets. Yeah, it's tough making a long relationship last, but what do we have other than trying to make it work?" He paused. "What else is there?

"You might think going after this girl is crazy. It's not. You should." He wagged an affirming finger in the air.

Stan nodded.

"You had a terrible loss, but maybe it's time to start doing something. Right?"

What else did he have? Nothing. Closing his eyes, he pictured June's warm smile. He opened his eyes a moment later. Something gray moved near the shoulder of the road. "Deer!" he shouted.

The animal hesitated and then, as though denying the car's existence, started to cross. Dale turned the wheel and started over the centerline. The deer kept coming.

Stan grabbed the wheel and pulled it so they were headed right for the deer.

"What are you—" Dale started. He fought against Stan's pulling, but then relented.

They reached the spot where the deer had been. It was gone. It had kept running across the road. Dale hit the brakes.

Stan turned and caught a glimpse of the deer's white tail disappearing into the black woods.

The Caddy idled on the right shoulder. They sat breathing heavily in the silence. Adrenaline welled up in Stan's mouth and, thinking of them, he shook another cigarette from his pack. He pushed the lighter in.

"Thanks," Dale said. "I would have hit it..." He exhaled. "I'm sorry. I didn't...I didn't know what you were doing."

"It's just instinct to steer away from them like you did. Almost everybody does," Stan said, trying to comfort him. "But my dad hammered it into my head that if they're moving, you head right towards them. They won't be there by the time you are." It was the kind of advice that always seemed wrong, but worked. Like steering into a skid. Or pilots getting out of a tailspin by turning into it. Backing up a trailer, turning the opposite direction from the way you want the trailer to go.

"I hate those goddamn things." Dale nodded. "They just blind-side you like that...out of nowhere. You'd think they'd see the lights. They must see the lights. Why the hell do they cross?" He seemed to want Stan to give him an answer.

Stan took a long drag on his cigarette. "They must think they can make it. Maybe they misjudge because of the light. Maybe they don't know it's a car. There's nothing like cars in the natural world. Cars haven't been around long enough for deer to evolve a defense."

"Let me have a puff of that," Dale said. He brought the ciga-rette to his lips. Exhaling, he shifted into drive and pulled back onto the road. He took another drag and then handed it back. Gravel crunched under the tires. "The problem is that the sonsabitches have no natural predators. We cleaned out the wolves, and now it seems like we're restricting the hunters more and more every year."

Stan nodded, simmering in adrenaline and nicotine.

Dale drove slowly at first. After a few miles, he got back up to speed. "All right, let's get you into town so you can see this girl."

Stan looked ahead at the shoulders. Glad to have a job, spotting deer. He flicked his cigarette out the window and turned around to watch the sparks explode and disappear.

Chapter VII

The houses and mailboxes along the road became less scattered and slowly became Gaylord. Dale followed the streets of a quiet neighborhood. Most of the houses were dark, except for porch lights and the occasional motion-sensing light that Dale's Caddy set off. They passed a lone figure on the sidewalk—probably a teenager straggling home. Stan imagined the young man turning the cold doorknob of his parents' house as quietly as possible, hoping the dog wouldn't bark, hoping just to make it into bed without anyone waking to notice the time or the smell of beer. Stan had dreaded the time that Shannon would be pushing the limits of her own curfew, but tonight he felt closer to the teenagers than he did the parents. May they lie in their beds, staring into the darkness, recalling whatever chances they had taken. He wanted for them the bliss of knowing they had gotten away with it at least for one night. He touched the pack of cigarettes in his pants pocket and felt young.

Dale turned onto the main drag. The roadside brightened with the luminous parking lot lights of gas stations and all-night restaurants. Stan looked ahead and tried to guess what building might be the hospital. Nothing was familiar to him. Gaylord was bigger than he imagined it would be. More traffic. How would he find June's street? A cab? Nope—he had no money. The hospital could be miles from her place. He couldn't ask Dale to drive him to June's. He'd already done enough. Pushing down a rising fear, he tried to put together a plan. Any phonebook would have a map of the town. But what if she didn't even live in town? Or, what if she wasn't even in the book? "Can you just drop me off at one of these gas stations?" he asked.

Without a word, Dale flipped his turn signal, slowed, and then turned off of the road. He'd probably had enough. Stan lit another cigarette.

"Are you going to be all right?" Dale asked. "I'm really sorry about not getting you shoes." He touched the hook in his ear.

"I'll be fine. I've got tough feet." He opened his door and stepped out. The wind had died down. "Thanks for everything, and take care of that ear."

"Just take care of yourself and get back on track."

"I'll try," he said. "And thanks again." He closed the door and took a long drag.

The taillights on Dale's Caddy eventually disappeared. Stan smoked his cigarette. The smell of fast food wafted around him. Broke, no car, no shoes—trying to see June seemed ridiculous to him. He flicked the spent butt across the parking lot. Dale's words echoed in his head. Turning it in his hand, he finally pushed the pack of cigarettes down into his front pocket.

The fluorescent lights hummed in the canopy above him. Ephorons were among the insects bumping against the long, thin bulbs. Starting toward the gas station doors, he wondered what they were doing way out here, so far from the river.

He stood in the doorway. The young man behind the cash register was probably eighteen or nineteen. His long bang covered his left eye and he had at least three earrings in his left ear. He nodded his head rhythmically. A manic guitar solo whined from a radio near the cash register. The store itself glowed under the fluorescent lighting.

A few seconds passed. The kid looked over. His face paled. It was as though he was thinking, okay, this is it, this is the night they warn you about. This is the nut with the gun and the hollow eyes.

Stan probably looked pretty deranged with his wild beard, wiry hair, bare feet, and odd clothes. Probably looked like some kind of castaway. "I just need to know if you have a phonebook," he said.

Looking him over, the kid nodded.

"I'm not coming in because I don't have shoes on. Isn't that a rule?"

The kid nodded again. His eyes seemed to find the words on Stan's sweatshirt, and the corners of his mouth rose slightly.

"Okay then, could you just toss the phonebook to me?" He rubbed his upper lip and smelled the stale smoke and nicotine on his fingers, an old smell that brought him back to his youth.

The kid studied him for a second. Then he grinned. "Look, I don't care about you being barefoot, man," he said. "Come on in. Phonebook's over there hanging beneath the payphone. It's chained to the wall, so I couldn't throw it to you even if I wanted to."

Stan thanked him and stepped into the bright light. Candy bars, fishing poles, gum, beach balls, sunglasses, engine coolant—everything—shined beckoningly. The smell of the rotisserie hotdogs overwhelmed the place and instantly reminded him of his first job as a cashier at a Seven Eleven.

The kid stepped down from behind the counter. He pointed to the phone. "Right there," he said. He walked toward a door near the back.

Stan watched him.

The kid disappeared and then returned, wheeling a mop and bucket. He wrung out the mop and passed it over the floor in front of the entrance. He went to the backroom again and came out with a yellow sign that warned people about the slippery floor.

Stan flipped through the pages of the phonebook. She'd be in the Ts, but he started somewhere in the Ss and worked his way slowly. He didn't know what he'd do if he didn't find her address. He wasn't exactly sure what he'd do even if he *did* find her. The kid pushed the mop here and there in the aisles.

Reaching the Ts, he looked for Thorpe, but soon his finger was passing over Thume, Thumm, Thumma, Thumme. His mouth went dry. But, passing through the Th's again, he found it: Thorpe, J 721 Middle St. He held his finger on it for a moment, took a deep breath, and then released it. "Hey," he said, "How far is Middle Street from here?"

The kid, returning from the back of the store, looked up toward the ceiling. "I'd say about five miles, I think." He ran his hand through his hair and then dropped it under the collar of his shirt. He scratched between his shoulders. "Yeah," he nodded, "five miles."

"Oh shit." It felt tight when he tried to take a breath. Five miles. Barefoot. In a town he didn't even know? He let the phonebook fall out of his hands and it banged against the wall.

"What's wrong?"

Stan looked at him. "Nothing." He would have to call her. He couldn't walk five miles. He reached deep into both pockets, already knowing that there wouldn't be change in either. He looked at the kid. "Do you have a phone I could make a local call on?"

The kid studied him for a moment. "I'm not supposed to," he started. He dropped down behind the counter and came back up. He set a phone on the counter top. "Just go ahead," he said. He walked over to the radio and turned down the loud music.

Stan thanked him. Picking up the base of the phone, he carried it as far as the cord would let him. Out of the blue he was calling her at eleven at night. It wasn't what he'd wanted, but then it might be better than just showing up on her doorstep. He didn't have many choices. He couldn't ask to sleep on the kid's couch. He punched in her number.

She picked up after the fifth ring and answered sleepily.

"June?" His heartbeat was in his throat. He tried to swallow it.

Her end of the line was quiet for a moment. "Who is this?" She sounded uneasy. "Alan, I hope this isn't you. I told you—"

"It's Stan Carter," he said. "I came into town. I'm in Gaylord."

"Stan? Are you all right? Why are...Why did you dive in like that? Why are you calling me?"

He searched for words. "I'm calling," he started. "I'm calling because I wanted to tell you that I'm sorry."

Silence. "It's almost eleven o'clock. I'm in bed. I don't—"

"That's not the only reason I'm calling," he said. "I'm sorry it's so late, but I just needed to call you. I needed to talk to you."

The kid turned around with a deposit bag and crouched to spin the dial on a small safe.

"You swim away like that and now you—" she started.

"Can I see you?"

"What? Can you see me?"

"I just want to see you and talk. If we could just talk. When I dove in and swam away, I wasn't thinking right. But I see now that I can't keep running away. I just think it would be good if we talked." He switched the phone to his other ear. He wiped his palm against his pants. "I'm just talking about talking."

"You're in Gaylord?" she asked.

"Yes."

Another moment of silence. "I can't talk about anything right now. Not right now. We can talk tomorrow. Come by Lenders One tomorrow. It's in the book."

"June," he pleaded. "I want to talk to you tonight. I need to...it's just that I came into town."

"It's eleven," she said. "You can talk to me tomorrow. But you'll have to come by Lenders One."

"June?"

"What?"

"I like you. I really do. I mean, not...I mean, I think I could like...I'm so sorry that I just dove in like that. I'm sorry. I really do like you or at least...I wish I wouldn't have done that. I wish..."

"Stan," she said. "We'll talk tomorrow. I'm really tired. But, I will talk to you tomorrow. I'm glad that you called and I know that you're okay. I didn't understand—"

"Okay," he said, "We'll talk tomorrow. I'll come by."

"Okay. I'll see you tomorrow."

"But couldn't we just talk tonight? Couldn't I—"

"No," she said. "I'll talk to you tomorrow. The office is right downtown. I'm going to go back to sleep now. Goodnight."

Stan stayed on the line, but didn't say anything.

"I said 'goodnight,' Stan."

"Okay. Goodnight. I'll see you tomorrow." He hung up the phone and set it back on the counter. His vision blurred. Leaning against the humming ice machine, he tried to imagine what to do next. He had only one option. He had to go to her house. She couldn't turn him away. He could tell her that he'd hitchhiked into town. That's how badly he had wanted to see her. He thought about it. It would probably scare her more than anything. But, what otherwise?

He wished he were still at the cabin, maybe sleeping next to her, waiting for whatever the next day would bring. He saw himself in the river diving away from her. "Shit," he said.

"What's up now?"

"What?...Oh, nothing. I just need to get to Middle Street."

"Dude, are you on foot?"

Embarrassed, he nodded.

The kid looked at the clock. It read ten minutes to eleven.

Stan started towards the door. "Can you give me a general idea where Middle Street is?"

The kid scratched his chin. "You can't walk all that way barefoot, man."

Stan puffed out his cheeks and exhaled. "I don't have a lot of choice."

The kid glanced at the clock again. "Look, the third shift guy replaces me at eleven. If you want to wait I can give you a ride."

Stan swallowed. "I can't give you anything for gas or anything. It'd be pure charity."

Nodding, the kid opened the register and started counting ones. "Not a problem. My folks' house ain't too far from Middle Street."

A few minutes before eleven, a man about Stan's age came in wearing a polo shirt identical to the kid's. His brown hair was streaked with gray. He looked around the place and paused for a moment at the sight of Stan. He held a thick paperback book. The bookmark looked to be about twenty pages in. He wore a wedding ring.

"Chris," he started. "Are you kidding me? You didn't put up that new sun glasses display?"

Chris pressed his time card into the punch clock. It thunked heavily. "It was busy tonight," he said. "Windy, too. It took me forever to change the gas prices. The numbers were blowing all over the parking lot, dude."

"Busy my ass. I bet the can smells like weed, though, doesn't it? You had time to toke a doobie, didn't you?"

Stan smirked at the word doobie. Still, he knew what the man was feeling. Poor guy had been hoping to come to work and have a decent night. A good night. Maybe even have a moment or two to himself just to think or not think. Or, some time to knock out a few pages from his book. Stan had tried to take up reading himself, but never really had the time or concentration to finish a novel. At home there'd been no time, and the guys in the break room, with their swearing and smoking, didn't exactly give the place the feel of a library. If he read for too long, ignoring them, they turned their teasing on him. "What are you, Carter, a big shot now? Trying to impress management or what? Or are you reading the story of two gay Irish lovers. Patrick FitzMichael and Michael FitzPatrick." Not wanting to alienate himself from his co-workers, he closed the book. "Just trying to keep from going brain dead, I guess," he'd say. "Brain dead's okay," a co-worker once said, "Keeps you from thinking too much. Don't want to think in a place like this."

He knew exactly what this guy wanted. He didn't want to pick up Chris' slack, some kid who had no idea what it was like to have a family and to have nearly every minute of his life accounted for. Stan knew what it was like being disappointed by the laziness of the previous shift. He had hated coming into work when the shift before hadn't finished their quota or recalibrated their machines.

"I don't smoke pot," Chris shot back. "I can't help what the customers do in the john."

"Yeah, I'll bet it's the customers. Look, just stay and put up the display and I won't tell Paul how much you're screwing around on your shift. I've got to do inventory tonight, and the display needs to go up before tomorrow. I can't do both." He stepped up behind the register and looked at some papers.

"Dude, you'll have to put up the display. I got to give this poor soul a ride." He motioned towards Stan.

The other man looked. His eyes dropped down to the words on Stan's sweatshirt. He smirked as he looked away. "I'm going to have to tell Paul. He's not going to be happy. Every night it's something with you. If it's not—"

"So tell him," Chris said, "I really don't care. I'm putting in my two-week notice tomorrow anyway, dude. I'm heading up north for college." Chris pointed west.

Stan admired Chris' cockiness, though not his sense of direction.

The other man didn't say anything for a moment. "Let me get this right, *you're* going to college?"

Chris nodded and grinned. "Graphic design, man. I'm going to be *designing* sunglasses displays for guys like you to put up."

The other man didn't say anything. He seemed distracted by some thought. He ran his hand over his face. "Chris Jackson in college. That's quite an image. Smoking dope and skipping class...you'll be back here with your tail between your legs by November," he said, but his voice sounded deflated. He picked up a sprayer of glass cleaner from under the counter.

Stan guessed what the other man was feeling. He was jealous of the kid because he seemed to be on the way somewhere—young kid who didn't really have to care about inventory or displays. Chris didn't know enough to really value the freedom that he had. Stupid fucking bang hanging in his eyes. Stan had met kids like him on the line. They'd come in for a summer, talk in the break room about the University of Michigan or Michigan State, and then vanish into a hopefulness that felt out of reach for most of the guys. He wondered what those kids were doing with their lives. Probably lawyers or doctors.

"No way, dude. I'm not going to work in a place like this for the rest of my life," Chris laughed, good-naturedly.

Stan followed the kid to the door. He probably hadn't meant to be cruel, but the words still carried a sting. He probably couldn't imagine that some people did work in places like this for the rest of their lives. His brain, pumped up on what seemed like invulnerability, couldn't let such a dark thought in.

The older worker looked at Chris and Stan. He pinned on his nametag indicating that he was Larry. Night Supervisor. "Fuck you, then," Larry sighed, rubbing his eyelids with his fingers, "Just get the hell out of here so I can get some work done. Someone's got to keep this place running." He probably wanted the last sentence to be full of pride. It sounded more pitiful than anything.

Following Chris out to his car, Stan knew that the inventory *and* the display would be done by morning. The bookmark wouldn't move. After his shift, just after dawn, he'd drive home red-eyed, brush the hair of a sleeping child, slip into bed with his wife, and sleep the day away. Sleep the rest of his life away. Or maybe take a shower and put on his uniform for his day job.

Chapter VIII

Chris focused on driving as they cruised down the main street. He flipped the turn signal deliberately, held his hands at ten and two, and seemed to draw himself tight against the driver side door. Was the kid second-guessing his decision to give some crazy-looking stranger a ride?

"You in a band?" Stan asked, trying to put Chris at ease. There was an amplifier and guitar case in the backseat.

"Yeah. Just a local band. FTS, man."

"FTS?"

"Yeah, that's the name of my band. Fight the System. Or, Fuck the System. Fondle the Salami. Whatever you like. We do originals, so we don't get to play out much. But, I couldn't be in no cover band, dude, playing other peoples' songs. Popular shit. In a town like this, that's where the money is. But, you end up in a golf course clubhouse playing 'Cheeseburger in Paradise'. Quietly, too, so the golfers can talk about their new putters." He eased back into his seat and took a hand off the wheel.

"Has your band ever played in front of people?" Stan had a guitar when he was in high school, but only mastered three chords.

"We have at parties—one where there was about two hundred people. That was one of the best nights of my life. People dancing, jumping all over the place to music we were making. The music was the blood of that night. I mean, if we would have stopped, they'd have stopped. And, if we'd kept going all night, they would have too. It was better than sex."

Everything was dark. No streetlights. Hunched and gray, houses ticked past on either side of the road. They'd weathered many winters.

Chris lit a cigarette, exhaled, and an earthy odor filled the car. Though it'd been a long time, Stan knew the smell immediately.

"You want a hit, man?" Chris asked, still inhaling. He held the joint towards Stan.

"No, thanks."

Chris took another long drag. "Well, just say when." He inhaled, holding the smoke. Then he pushed a cassette into the tape deck. Guitar, bass, and drums, crammed together and racing, accompanied the barking shout of the singer. Stan could only make out the words "Fuck off."

"How long have you wanted to do graphic design?" he asked, raising his voice above the music. Chris was going nearly thirty-five miles an hour.

"What?"

"Didn't you say you're going to study graphic design?"

Chris took another hit and, a few seconds later, exhaled his answer. "That sounded as good as anything else." He drummed his thumbs on the wheel to the beat.

"What do you mean?" Stan rolled down his window and tapped out a cigarette.

"My folks said they'd help out with school if I had some kind of major in mind, so I picked graphic design." He put the joint to his mouth again and the tip flared.

Eyes glowed from the side of the street. When they passed where the eyes had been, there was only a garbage can. Probably a raccoon.

"You sure you don't want a hit of this? You look like the kind of guy who likes to go to the kingdom now and again."

"No, really, I'm fine."

Chris shrugged and turned onto another street.

"Do you know anything about it?" Stan slid against the passenger door as Chris slowed imperceptibly to take the corner.

"About what?"

"Graphic design."

"Not really. I guess it's kind of like art with computers." He straightened the wheel.

Stan flicked an ash out the window. The night air rushed in cool, almost chilling. "But why did you pick graphic design if you don't know anything about it?" He motioned his thumb towards the backseat. "Why not music?"

"And play what?" Chris asked. "Classical guitar? They don't

teach punk or grunge. And, if they did, I don't think they could teach me anything." He turned the music down. "I know punk. I know grunge."

"I mean, the way you talked about music, the way you talked about playing for an audience, it just seems like you'd—"

"Hey, look," Chris interrupted, "I picked graphic design so my folks would help fund school. I can't float it on my own. My girlfriend's heading up for a nursing degree, and I want to go with her."

Girlfriend. Of course. Stan had taken his job on the line so many years ago because he and Rachel were getting serious. He sure as hell hadn't had anything like music to be passionate about. He wasn't really passionate about anything at Chris' age. Why was this young guy so willing to walk away from it?

"How long have you been seeing her?"

"About seven months now."

Stan took another drag from his cigarette. "But what about your band?"

"What about it? Gaylord's not exactly Seattle."

"What about the town where the college is?" he asked determinedly. "Couldn't you be in a band there?"

"It's a piss hole town like this. No music scene. At least not a scene for the kind of music I want to play."

Stan dropped his cigarette out the window and then rolled it up. "I just think you should…maybe you *could* go to Seattle."

"Stacy's not in Seattle." Chris took another hit.

"But, you'll give up music like that? It just seems—" Stan's voice was going higher.

"I'm not giving it up…not for her. I just can't do it. Do you know how many bands there are like mine out there, man? Do you know how many of them make it? Not many," he exhaled.

Outside of the headlights, the dark neighborhoods were all around them. Stan felt like he used to feel when he would try to argue with his father. With only adolescent passion on his side, he'd make his case against logic and experience. He had no idea why he was pushing the kid. "I just think that if you love music, you should at least get a band going up north. Maybe then—"

"Maybe what?" Chris asked, "Maybe a record producer will be deer hunting, hear us, and then want to sign us? You sound like our drummer. You can't go half ass like that. It's either all or nothing. That is if you're trying to make it."

The kid had an answer for everything. "But why choose nothing?" Stan asked, his voice cracking slightly. "Why not *all*? If you don't—if you quit now. Then, later, it's harder, probably impossible."

"Look," Chris explained, "I already know that music is going nowhere for me, dude. I can live with that. Stacy's the best thing that's ever happened to me. I can't walk away from that to go after something that's never going—"

"Stop!" Stan yelled, suddenly seeing the immensity.

Chris hit the brakes. They slowed, but still slammed into a tree that lay across the road. Pain radiated from Stan's forehead and down into his neck.

A silence that could have been a second or an hour settled around them. Something rang quietly, stubbornly, in Stan's head.

"Holy shit, dude," Chris finally said. "Are you okay? Where did…whoa, look at the windshield! Is your head all right?"

Chris sounded funny, as though he were talking into a can. Stan pulled his hands away from his head. The pain doubled.

"Your forehead's bleeding. Are you okay?"

Lifting his head, Stan squinted into the splintered windshield. Tiny cracks spread out from the center of the spot where his head had struck. The tree trunk, a long shadow in front of the car, was at least four feet around. Where did it come from? Warm liquid ran into his left eye. The pain throbbed.

Chris pressed something into his hand. "Use this t-shirt, man. You're really bleeding."

Stan pressed the cloth into his eye and then against his forehead. He looked through the windshield again.

"Say something, dude."

Stan held the bloody t-shirt open. He made out large letters across the front. "This is one of your band t-shirts." Blood dribbled into his eye again.

"Don't worry about it," Chris said. He reached over and lifted Stan's hand and the t-shirt back to his forehead. "The t-shirts were our drummer's idea. Are you sure you're okay, man?"

"How did we hit a tree? It doesn't make sense." Eyes closed, he saw tiny lightning flash across his eyelids.

"I don't know," Chris said. "Fucking out of nowhere."

Stan could barely open his eyes against the pain of his headache. He held the t-shirt tightly against the wound.

"Sit tight, dude. I got to check out the car."

Stan shook his head. "I'll get out, too. I want to stand."

They opened their doors. "Man, that thing's huge."

Dizzy, Stan leaned against the car door as soon as he closed it. "How did it get here?" he asked himself more than Chris. Past the sidewalk, in the middle of a yard, almost two feet of the base of the tree was still rooted in the ground. On the other side of the street, the leafy branches of the treetop lay in another yard. It hadn't hit anything on its way down. "The wind must have brought it down. Must have been all rotted on the inside." He studied the fallen trunk.

Chris climbed onto it and balanced as though it were a surfboard. "This bad boy could have fallen right on us." He flicked a lighter and relit the roach.

"For Christ's sake, put that thing out," Stan said. He tied the t-shirt around his head.

Chris jumped down and examined the grill of his car. "Oh shit, man. The front end is totaled."

Stan looked at the smashed headlights. His vision went in and out of focus.

"Is everybody okay?" a voice called out.

Most of the porch lights of nearby houses had come on. Under some, figures in bathrobes moved around. One spoke into a cell phone.

"Put out the joint," Stan hissed. Holding it between his hands, he set his head on the hood of the car, trying to squeeze out some of the pain.

Chris slumped down against the driver side door. "I totaled the car." The small ember glowed between his fingers.

For a while they both sat quietly. From time to time Chris inhaled. Stan's pain lessened. Other voices called out to them. Neither answered.

"I can't fucking believe it," Chris whispered. "The fucking car."

From the corner of his vision, Stan noticed a set of headlights turn from a side street toward them. Chris stood up. The car moved slowly, and the two of them glowed brighter and brighter in the growing light. Then everything began to flash red and blue.

"Oh, fuck." Chris said.

"Get rid of the joint," Stan hissed.

Chris dropped it and rubbed it out. What would this look like to the cops? They wouldn't see the truth. They'd see a barefoot bum with no ID riding with a stoned kid who just had a car accident. They'd have to take him in. He had nobody to call for bail. He could call June, but it wasn't exactly the way he wanted to see her again. She might not even come.

The police car stopped behind Chris' car. The doors opened. "Everybody okay?"

"He hurt his head," Chris said, pointing to Stan.

Both cops looked at Stan.

"I'm okay," he said. Something he'd felt earlier on the river, after all of June's questions, rushed through him again. The police would have their own questions. Too many questions.

An officer moved closer. "Let me take a look at it."

Stan bolted. He vaulted over the tree trunk and, once out of the light, ran for the nearest yard. His vision blurred, but he could make out the yards and houses around him. One of the officers shouted for him to stop.

Pain pulsed in waves in his head. He ran through a few front yards and soon spotted a house with thick bushes beneath a picture window. Branches rubbed against him as he pressed himself between the bushes and the house. Leaning back, he rested his shoulder blades against the bottom-most pieces of aluminum siding. They made a tinny, buckling sound that sent his heart leaping.

He had to tighten his stomach and breathe through his nose to hold back laughs. Had he inhaled Chris' second-hand smoke? He should be scared, but more than anything he felt charged, like fighting a big fish on the river. Maybe it was shock.

Wherever it'd come from, his giggling died immediately when a searchlight started down the street. It swept across a yard, across the street, and then across another yard. Then back. It was moving towards him. There was a second light. It wasn't long and it didn't sweep. It seemed aimed more at the ground and up closer to the houses—an officer searching behind the bushes with a flashlight. Stan looked again. A second set of flashing blue and red lights had joined the first.

They'd spot him if he ran. They'd find him if he stayed put. It was bad that he'd run in the first place.

His eyes adjusted to the darkness. A few feet from him he could make out where the porch butted up against the house. He reached towards the blackness. His hand kept going. He went headfirst, and crawled under the porch. The dirt was cold, but he dragged himself in. He edged his way into the space beneath the stairs and laid his head on the ground. He would have to sit and be quiet. Either they would find him or they wouldn't.

Five minutes later there were footsteps.

The bushes shished together. Light flashed briefly off the brick of the foundation. Something was working Stan's heart like a speed bag.

"Anything?" a voice called from the street.

"No." The voice came from above Stan. Slivers of flashlight shone through the steps. His heartbeat echoed back to him in the dirt. Footsteps clicked up the driveway.

"All right kid," the officer shouted. "You might as well come out."

Stan didn't move.

"Your buddy already told us who you are and where you live.

There's really no point to hiding."

Chris couldn't have told them anything. He only knew about Middle Street.

"Come out now, and it will be easier on you."

He needed to wait them out, but he didn't want to wait all night. He had to get to June's. What seemed like another minute or two passed.

"I'm going back to the car," the distant voice shouted.

"Hold up, I'll go back with you."

The scraping of their feet on the blacktop and their muffled talking soon disappeared. Stan waited. The whole announcement about going back to the car could have been a trick, something to lure him out.

Time passed. The cold crept up from the ground and into his bones, settling deeper than any shivering could relieve. His head simmered in its own dull pain. Crickets began to chirp around the house. Stretching his back, he ran through everything that he'd been trying to do, and everything that had happened to him that night. It ended with him hiding from the police under a stranger's porch. He tried to laugh, but what came out was more like a sob. What would Rachel say if she could see him?

His life with them had been so simple. He worked, he paid bills, he watched television when he wasn't repairing something on the house. Since Shannon had been an infant, Stan had given up trying to fulfill any of his own desires. If he tried to do something for himself, it usually cost him. Usually he paid in guilt. Sometimes more. A memory came to him. It had happened years ago, before Shannon was even a year old. He remembered the fool he'd been and maybe still was.

Chapter IX

This isn't going to work," Rachel declared. Stan had heard the tone before. He knew that they were going home. The day had never cooled as he had hoped. He lay in his underwear on top of his sleeping bag, though the heat didn't really bother him. The assembly line was always hot. He could sleep through just about anything. Rachel often scolded him for not waking up at night when Shannon was crying.

For the past hour he had been trying to follow the gist of conversations floating in from other campsites. He wished he could be with the other campers sharing in their light laughter. He imagined himself on the river, felt water around his legs and saw the dark bends and holes where he would cast and retrieve his spinners and draw trout out of their hiding. Closing his eyes, he even listened for the sound of the river, the sound of its constant movement.

He strained to ignore the baby and Rachel. Even with his back to them he knew his wife was trying to nurse Shannon. A swishing sound came from the sleeping bag where Shannon shook her head rooting for milk. Her throat sucked and clicked at the air. "It's right here," Rachel cooed at first, then stated, then hissed from between her teeth. Shannon latched on a few times, but soon the infant's dry sucking noises filled the tent again. "You had it," Rachel said, "What's wrong, Angel?"

It felt as though this had gone on for hours.

"I'm not going to do this all night," she said, this time a little louder.

"What's wrong?" he asked, rolling towards her. Her back was to him and she lay on top of her sleeping bag in her bra and panties. He rubbed her shoulder.

"Your hand's hot."

He pulled it away.

"She nurses for a little bit, then falls asleep, then wakes up. It's been like this for the past hour. She just won't fill herself. It's too hot for her to eat. I think something is wrong."

He rolled to his back and looked up into the blue darkness of the tent. He hadn't prepared himself for these kinds of sacrifices. Broken nights of sleep, holding her for her naps, diaper changes. All of these things he had expected. His friends had teased him so much that when the moments finally came they weren't nearly as bad as he'd anticipated. But he'd never expected Rachel to become a hypochondriac on the baby's behalf. For her everything was a sign of illness or a cause for panic. Sneezing too much. Spitting up too much. Not nursing enough. Too much gas. Strange crying. They'd been to the pediatrician eight times since Shannon was born, not including the required visits. Of the eight times, only one had turned out to be anything. An ear infection. The doctor's diagnosis explained away a night filled with inconsolable crying, both the baby and Rachel. But then again it really hadn't been anything. Drops. All it had taken were a few prescription drops and Shannon had become her old self again. When would Rachel be herself again? A baby—one addition to the family. She changed everything.

He heard Shannon latch on again and a coolness rushed through him. Maybe this time she would stay on, fill her tummy, and get some sleep.

"I think we should go home," Rachel sighed.

Laughter rose from a nearby campsite. They weren't laughing at him, but it felt like it. He was jealous—jealous of their ease, jealous of the beers he imagined they'd been sipping, jealous of how for this one night they could think of nobody else but themselves. They would be here in the morning.

"Stan?"

"Home? Are you sure?" he asked. His voice was high, almost pleading. "That's two hours in the van. I bet it's going to cool off. If we stay here we could leave in the morning."

"When in the morning?" she asked, "When you get back from fishing?"

Could she actually read his thoughts? "No," he said, "Christ, no. We'll get up, see how Shannon is doing, and—"

A cry exploded out of his daughter and he jumped. The murmur of a nearby campsite stopped.

"What, Angel? What is it? Does your tummy hurt?" There was a wavering in Rachel's voice that he knew. She was close to crying.

Her elbow rose up from her side. He had seen this before, too—a familiar image from many nights. She was trying to guide her nipple into Shannon's mouth, trying to help her latch on. Sometimes it worked.

He couldn't believe they were going to leave. He had worked like a lawyer to argue the idea. She laughed when he said that the change of scenery would do her good. "Don't think this has anything to do with me," she said. Though he refused to agree with her, he didn't pursue that line of reasoning for long. Instead he argued that *he* needed a break, a break from ten-hour days in the plant. He reminded her how hard he worked. "We've been on mandatory overtime for a month and a half. I just need a little break." She understood, she said, but it worried her to be so far from the pediatrician, so far from any hospital. What if something were to happen? "Nothing's going to happen," he'd assured her. "Shannon's ten months old now." When she still hesitated he reminded her of the work he was doing at home.

"It's like I'm either handling engine parts, or dishes, or laundry, or diapers. Seems like the only thing I haven't handled in a while is you." He said this while smiling, joking. Through the joke he reminded her of everything he'd been doing around the house and everything they hadn't been doing in the bedroom. "I know, I know," she said. She broke and agreed to a one-night camping trip.

Stan shifted to try to find a more bearable position under the porch. His head throbbed from the impact with the windshield. Through his new pain, the pain of the old memory kept coming back. He pushed so hard, so selfishly. He'd been willing to take an infant on a camping trip. What made him so desperate?

"Stan, she won't eat," Rachel sobbed.

"All right, all right. I'll start the van and get the air going," he said. He zipped up his pants and then unzipped the door of the tent. The orange of other fires flickered around him. He started to break camp.

Later he could make out Rachel's silhouette waiting in the passenger seat of the minivan. Out beyond the minivan was a darkness to which his eyes barely adjusted. In that darkness four or five campfires burned and cast the shadowy movement of people around the flames. Not more than twenty feet away the orange of a cigarette glowed—someone working his way towards the outhouses.

He pulled up the last of the stakes. He broke down the collapsible poles. He hoped they'd both be asleep when he got in the van. If he couldn't fish, then what he wanted for the two-hour drive home was quiet—time to himself.

He opened the hatch to the van and threw the tent in. Rachel said something, but he closed it before he could make out what. It was something about Shannon.

He opened his door. Rachel sat crying in the sudden light from the overhead dome.

"Come on, Rachel. What's wrong now?" A wet stain darkened the front of her shirt. His voice softened. "What's wrong?"

"It's Shannon. She was eating and then she threw up everything." She was almost screaming.

"She's spit up before." In the back, Shannon seemed to be resting well in her car seat. He ducked under the tip of his fishing pole and closed the door to extinguish the light. The last thing he wanted was Shannon to wake up.

"This wasn't spit up. She threw up. And she feels like she's boiling," Rachel sobbed.

His body tensed. In the past ten months he'd heard Rachel crying too many times. Before that he'd never heard it. "She seems fine now," he said, reaching to put the back of his hand against Shannon's forehead, as his own mother had always done to him. Despite his reassuring words, he worried. Shannon's forehead felt like a piece of metal that'd just come off a grinder. The heat surprised him. Something hot went up his spine like mercury in a thermometer.

"What?" Rachel asked. "She is hot, isn't she?"

They were two hours from any hospital. They were a good ten minutes from a paved road. "She does feel warm," he finally admitted.

Lying under the porch, shivering, Stan tried to wince away the rest of the memory. He thought about coming out from the darkness. It had been long enough. The cops had to be gone. As he thought it, he heard a car go by. A police car? Probably not. Still, he couldn't take a chance. He settled into his spot, waiting and, though he fought them, details from the fishing trip continued haunting him.

Early that afternoon Rachel had asked him to feel Shannon's forehead. He'd felt the heat then too, but couldn't admit it.

"Doesn't she feel warm to you?" she'd asked.

"We've had her in the sun too much. Just stay in the shade," he had said, reeling a lighter test line onto his pole.

"But it doesn't feel like heat *on* her skin," she'd said. "It feels like heat *under* her skin. It feels like a fever."

He told her that things would get better as it got towards evening.

Turning in her seat, she reached back and set her hand on Shannon's forehead. "She's burning up." Her voice was concerned. Reproachful, too.

He rubbed his eyelids. He didn't know what to say. Guilt squirmed in him.

"Just go," she said, "At least she's asleep. Put the air on high and just drive." She stayed turned around in her seat, studying Shannon, touching the back of her fingers to her cheeks.

He shifted into drive and followed the two-track that circled around past the campsites. The fires were burning high. The silhouettes around them gestured, leaned forward, stabbed sticks into the coals. His headlights passed over them. The men waved. At other sites the fires had already been abandoned and had burned down to a soft orange. Dim lights glowed in the windows of pop-ups and RVs. Shadows moved inside.

They pulled out from the campsite. Rachel faced forward again, staring into the dark windshield. He was too ashamed to ask her what she was thinking and he guessed that he already knew. He focused on the dirt road snaking its way into the halo of his head-lights. Ruts and washouts made the driving difficult and he lost himself in the immediacy of the task. His fishing pole bounced and rattled in his ear. Rachel turned around a few more times. By the time they reached the pavement her head was resting against the passenger window.

Stan tilted his mirror. Shannon slumped into a sleeping position that would surely leave a kink in any adult's neck. She had a little smile. Stan shook his head, thankful that she was sleeping. Suddenly, she lurched forward and vomited down the front of herself. She whined faintly and fell asleep again.

The blackness outside constricted itself around the van as though it would even extinguish the illumination of their head-lights. Stan knew what he had to do, but feared it. He reached over and shook Rachel's leg. His own forehead felt hot. He held the steering wheel like a branch he was trying to snap. "Rachel," he said and nearly choked on her name.

She stirred and then woke quickly, unbuckling her seatbelt and turning around to Shannon. "What?" she asked.

He didn't say anything, hoping she'd see for herself so he didn't have to hear himself say it.

"What, Stan? Why'd you wake me up?"

"She threw up again." A car coming towards them had its brights on. He flashed his own.

Rachel told him to pull over.

"What? Here? There's nothing around." The other driver didn't flip down to dims. When the car passed, the inside of the van blazed with light.

"Pull over," she said.

Her voice was determined and sure. It surprised him. He slowed onto the gravel.

She unbuckled the baby and lifted her up and into her lap. While lifting her shirt and bra, she elevated Shannon's feet. Her breast glowed dimly in the dashboard light. A drop of milk hung from the nipple, glistening. The breast was better than him; he knew it. It, at least, could do something. Shannon kept sleeping even as Rachel tried to nurse her.

He moved his hands towards them. "Is she all right?"

"I don't know." She didn't look at him. "I think she might have heat exhaustion."

Stan drew his hands back.

Rachel pinched Shannon. Stan winced. When she started crying, Rachel pressed her breast into her face again and she started to nurse. She was still nursing after a minute. "Start driving," Rachel ordered.

Ahead there was nothing—no glow of white that might be an all-night convenience store or a gas station. Above the noise of the engine and the rattling fishing pole, he could hear Shannon nursing. The sound calmed him. At the same time he waited for the awful vomiting.

Rachel reached into the darkness in front of the passenger's seat.

"What are you doing?" he asked.

She told him to keep driving but to stop if they came to some kind of store.

He drove. He watched her, too. She poured bottled water onto her sleeve and pressed it to Shannon's forehead.

"Is she going to be okay?"

"I don't know. Watch the road!"

He jerked the right tire off the shoulder and then simmered in his adrenaline. The circle of light from the headlamps looked small. He flipped his brights on. Breathing deeply through his mouth, he tried to shake the tight feeling around his ribs.

Rachel sighed, sounding relieved.

"What?"

"Her pulse is normal and she's clammy. That's good. I'm pretty sure that means no heat stroke." She poured more water on her sleeve. This time she let Shannon suck on it.

The yellow dashes flitted into the light and then disappeared under his side of the van. "How do you know all of this?" he asked.

"The book," she said.

The book. He always hated the book. He could picture the illustration on the cover of the mother holding an infant in a rocking chair. He'd seen Rachel reading it more times than he could count. If Shannon were sick, Rachel would read the book over and over, sometimes the same pages six and seven times, as though trying to find something she'd missed. If Shannon was healthy, she read the book casually, flipping through, concentrating on the childhood diseases and maladies that were sprinkled through the pages. "Oh my God, I wouldn't know what to do if that happened," she would say. She read passages to him about encephalitis, Lyme disease, meningitis, Reye's syndrome, lockjaw. "How would we have done it?" she'd say as she would start to read through the common birth defects. "I don't think we could have handled it." She read them aloud, emphasizing the related problems: autism, cerebral palsy, congenital heart defect, Down syndrome, deformation, malformation, spina bifida. She'd read for almost an hour, often driving herself to the verge of tears. "It's so sad," she'd say. Ten minutes with the book could make her desperate, panicked, even if there was nothing wrong with Shannon.

"The book," he repeated, nodding.

"Is that place open?" she asked.

Ahead, on the right side of the road, a light pole illuminated the gravel entrance to a tiny gas station. He careened towards the lights.

"Slow down, Stan!"

The van idled on the apron of the gas station. They were open, thank God. Shannon nursed in the blast of the air conditioning. When she stopped, Rachel dunked her pacifier in water and then let her suck it. She whispered to the baby.

"She's cooler now," she said. "I think she's going to be okay." She lifted her over and buckled her into her car seat.

Stan tried to relax like her, but couldn't. "What could have happened?" he asked when she turned to buckle herself in.

She didn't answer right away. "If it was heat stroke, she could have died," she started. "Heat exhaustion? I'm not sure, but I know it's bad too. Usually you need a doctor with infants. We're lucky. Shannon was lucky."

He felt cut. "We're lucky because of you," he said. "You knew what to do."

"You have to, Stan." She balled a sweatshirt and made a pillow to lean against the window.

Earlier that day, he'd checked Shannon's brow, recognizing but ignoring the heat because he wanted to fish. He took deep breaths but couldn't get enough air.

"I'm sorry," he said. He meant that he was sorry for lying about not feeling Shannon's fever.

She didn't say anything at first. "Do you mind if I sleep?" she finally asked. "I'm so tired."

"No, go ahead. Sleep." He looked in the rearview mirror. His daughter's face, sleeping, glowed softly in the dashboard light. He waited for more vomiting, crying, anything, but it didn't come. He looked over at his wife. How could she sleep? He envied the way she seemed to know that it was over, that everything was okay for now. He didn't feel like anything would ever be okay again. What he did or failed to do could hurt her, even kill her. It was a simple truth.

Checking Shannon one more time, he shifted into drive.

"Watch for deer," Rachel mumbled.

"I will."

His fishing pole rattled, and he grabbed it. Pulling down with his fingers and pushing up with his thumb, he snapped the tip off.

The road wound out of the darkness. He watched the shoulders. When Shannon sighed or moved at all, he jerked his vision back toward the rearview mirror. The small face was always there, glowing faintly. Despite the long day, he was awake. He felt like he had taken amphetamines, like he did when he worked midnights. His bed was less than an hour away. He didn't feel like he'd ever sleep soundly again.

Chapter X

After that fishing trip, he seldom did anything for his own enjoyment. He was too afraid of making a mistake. Once you had a child, he decided, your own life ended or at least slept. When he'd bought the cabin, he believed in his heart that it would be for all of them.

The cabin. In the blackness under the porch, he easily imagined himself there. Without lights, the darkness was thick. If June hadn't come, he'd be there, sleeping. Fishing in the early afternoon. Working the garden in the twilight. Carving or fishing again in the evening. And in all of it, slowing down to pay attention to things. Holding a brook trout to study the olive green markings curved through the dark green of its high side. Or cradling radishes in his palms, the red going into white going into stringy root. Running his hands through the lightness of whittled slivers of wood. He couldn't decide if it was stupid or wonderful. It was certainly better than his job at the assembly plant. Better than any job he'd ever had. Of every possibility that lay before him, the idea of going back to the cabin and the river was the most reassuring. But then what? Eviction? Losing everything? "What are you going to do now?" The cabin was fantasy. He had to remember that. June was real. She could be the start of him getting on track. Or not.

He thought about Chris, the boy's passion for music. In high school, Stan had only wanted to party and get laid. The only classes he ever paid attention to were his shop classes. In the others he managed to earn Cs and Ds—enough to get by. He envied his friends who got jobs in the plant and felt that he finally had arrived when he got his. New car. A little house. Family. How could he have known that it would turn into this? The job hadn't been that bad until he lost his reason for doing it. Running away to the cabin couldn't be much healthier. He didn't want to end up like Dale, full of regret, alone. Even Chris, a punk kid, could spot a pipedream. Stan had to choose reality. The bank wanted their money. The cabin wasn't his anymore.

Something many-legged crawled across his ear. He brushed it away. He'd waited long enough. He backed out from under the porch. Having been so long in the darkness, he saw clearly. He raised his head above the bushes and looked down the street toward the fallen tree. It was there, and beyond it the windshield and roof of Chris' car and the yellow lights of a wrecker, but nothing else. Shivering, he edged his way from behind the bushes and walked down to the street.

The porch lights were off. He hoped that people were back in their beds. It wasn't the safest route, but he stuck to the sidewalk. Besides the arrhythmic padding of his own feet, he heard nothing except the faint electrical hum of transformers overhead. It reminded him of nights on the cabin porch when, if he'd listen for it, he could hear the river moving. It was always there if he listened for it.

He was probably going in the wrong direction. At the first intersection, he found street signs. The cross street came into focus. "Henry Avenue," he said. The sign marking the street he was on read Middle Street. He smiled at his good luck. Maybe it was a sign. He laughed. He was on the four hundred block.

Whatever it looked like and however ringing its bell would change his life, her house was only three blocks away. He walked at first and then stumbled into a jog. When his head started throbbing, he slowed again to a walk.

Chapter XI

Silence. He stood in her front yard studying the small Cape Cod. What would he say when the bleary-eyed June opened the door? Everything about the house was neat, from the thick, manicured lawn to the trimmed hedges to the pillows on the porch swing. It looked as if it belonged to a married couple.

A cat crept from the side of the house. It jerked its head toward him and froze. "Here, kitty," he said just above a whisper, holding out his hand. It hissed and ran into the shadows.

How would he explain why he was there? Even he wasn't certain. The last time he was with her, he dove into a river and swam away. Here he was, at her house after midnight with a bloody shirt wrapped around his head. He'd simply tell her that he had to come. He had no other choice.

He touched the pack of cigarettes through his pants, knowing that a smoke would give him time to think. He had no matches, no light. For a moment, he thought it might be best just to try to sleep on her porch, maybe on the porch swing. Maybe if he woke before her, he would see what he was doing in a different light, and could slink away. He'd proposed to Rachel at one in the morning after tapping at her bedroom window. His first thought the next morning had been fear that he'd made a mistake.

This was no mistake. He started across the yard and up the porch stairs. They creaked. A few houses away, a dog barked a warning. Stan stopped. The dog couldn't have been barking at him. He continued to the door, sucking in a deep breath.

The doorbell glowed. He pressed it, and a faint bell responded inside. With no glass in the door for him to look through, he could only wait. He watched the windows around the house for light. Nothing. Maybe she hadn't heard it. Maybe she slept with the television on. Or, maybe she had heard it, and was on the phone to the police.

He pressed the doorbell again, holding it a little longer this time. After a moment, a window on his right lit up. He stepped back from the door and stood near the top of the porch stairs. He didn't want to startle her. When the porch light flashed into his face, he nearly fell backwards. He rubbed his eyes against the blinding brightness.

The door opened a moment later.

"Stan?"

He looked up, still squinting, still unable to open his eyes fully. Her blurred outline stood framed in the doorway. "It's me," he said.

The hazy, harsh light made her seem angelic. She wore a long sleeping t-shirt. Out of the bun, her hair hung past her shoulders.

"Your hair is pretty like that," he said.

She touched her hair. "Stan. What are you doing here?" She looked at him. "What happened to your head?"

"My head's fine." He stepped down onto the top step. From there he tried to look into her face, but still had to squint. "Could you turn off the porch light?"

Her arm disappeared in the house and then, for a moment, she disappeared in the absence of light. Then her silhouette faded in. Feeling dizzy, he sat down.

"Stan, are you all right?" Her voice was soft, concerned.

"I've just gotten used to the dark. The light was too much." His dizziness faded.

She stepped out onto the porch. The door creaked closed behind her.

"You must be cold," he said. "I mean, it can't be very warm in just a t-shirt." Her hips and breasts pressed against the thin material.

She crossed her arms over her chest. "What are you...I don't know...I don't understand why you're here. Why *are* you here?"

He tried to think of an answer that would make sense to both of them. He didn't want her to be afraid or angry.

"What happened to your head?" she asked. "It looks pretty bad."

"Just an accident on the way here. It looks worse than it feels." He wanted the conversation to stay this way, with simple questions that he could answer. He touched the t-shirt wrapped around his head. It was damp.

"An accident?"

"In a car," he said. "A kid was giving me a ride here, and we hit a tree. My head hit the windshield."

"Hit a tree? Was he drunk? How did you hit a tree?"

He held his face in his hands. No answers that he could give were simple. "It's too much to explain."

"Stan," her voice came again after a few seconds. "Why are you here? I don't understand any of this."

He lifted his face from his hands. She could have been angry. Seeing it was him, she could have simply not opened the door. She could have called the police the way he was acting. But no, she was caring about him, trying to figure him out. "Aren't you cold?" he asked. "I'm cold."

She rubbed her arms and looked out towards the street. She looked down at him. "I guess you can come in if you want."

He nodded. "I'd like to," he said. "I'd like to talk."

She opened the door and walked in. "Come in," she said. Her nipples pressed against her t-shirt.

He stood up and walked through the door.

Chapter XII

He sat on a couch in the front room aware of little else, though he was sure that there must be other things—a television, chairs, pictures, knick knacks. A clock ticked in another room. June came back in wearing a robe. She sat across from him. She'd turned on only one dim lamp.

"I'm sorry," he said after a moment.

"Stan, why—"

"I'm sorry I left you there like that at the river." He cleared his throat.

She didn't say anything for a moment. "You already told me that on the phone."

"That wasn't right," he said. "To leave you like that. I was scared." He listened to himself as though it were someone else talking.

"What do you mean?" she asked. "What were *you* scared of?"

"You're right," he interrupted. "It's pretty stupid for me to say that I was scared when you were the one left in the dark in a place you didn't know."

"I was more afraid for you," she said. "I waited for a while, but then I went back to my car. It wasn't hard to find. Maybe I would have been more afraid for myself if I hadn't been worrying about you. Why did you dive in like that?"

"I wasn't ready."

"For what?"

"Anything."

She moved in her seat. "Okay, so you're here now. Why did you come—"

"I think I'm ready to do it."

"Do what?"

"All of it."

"All of what? Stan—"

"All of it," he said. "Going to the bank. Stopping the foreclosure. Doing what I can to save the cabin."

Silence. June didn't move. He thought he could hear her house settling into its foundation. "I understand," he started, "If you can't now. I wouldn't blame you."

"I didn't say anything," she said. She pulled a pillow from behind her and hugged it against her front. "I'm pretty sure I can buy you some time with the bank. Then, you can move back to Farmington and get a job and—"

"I don't want to move back to Farmington."

"I don't understand. Don't you—"

"I guess I don't want the Farmington house," he managed.

"You don't want it? Why would you try to stop—"

"What if I price it to move? Can you buy me a couple months so I can just get rid of the place?" He couldn't tell if she wanted him in her house or not. "Farmington property is valuable real estate," he continued. "And most places aren't cheap. So, if I work with a realtor and price my place about twenty thousand below market value, it could sell in days."

She stood up and moved over to the couch next to him. "Why would you want to do that? If you priced it five thousand below value it would still move quickly."

"Not fast enough. I want to be rid of that place. I want to get started on whatever this new life is going to be." He set his hand on the couch cushion next to her leg. His smallest finger rested against her thigh. His blood shifted.

"I don't think you have to do that. You don't have to be so extreme. Let me talk to some people first and see what they say." She touched his knee, and he grabbed her hand and held it with both of his. Their palms were warm together. "I don't think you're thinking straight," she continued, "Everything that's happened, your head hitting the windshield—" She squeezed his hand. "You shouldn't make any quick decisions—you shouldn't—not about your house." She looked at him and their eyes locked.

His heart beat violently against his ribs. He began to speak, but had no idea what he was going to say. "I didn't just come here for that…about the house. I had to come. For you." He touched her cheek then drew his hand away. "I just thought that today there was something between us and I ran away from it. Swam away from it. And then I thought about you all night from the moment I got out of the river. I had to come to see if there was anything…if you felt anything or maybe thought…"

"What, Stan?"

"I just don't want to come off like I'm crazy."

She squeezed his hand again. "How do you mean?"

He took a breath. "It's just that I see you as a chance…to start again. I haven't wanted much in a while. I just think that this is good…that you could be good. I mean, if it comes to that. I need to try—"

She lifted his hand and kissed the tips of his fingers briefly. "I know what you're trying to say. I think I know what you're feeling."

Closing his eyes, he leaned forward. It felt to him as though he drifted in the darkness towards her for a long time. He wondered if she was backing away from his advance. Then their lips met. He kissed hungrily, devouring the kisses she gave back.

She dropped back into the couch, Stan leaning onto her. His erection rested against her thigh. He pressed against it. He kissed harder. He pressed harder, became animal, and he lost himself in the pleasure. Everything—the river, the cabin, the quest to get to June—dissolved in the world their closed eyes and searching lips made.

Then an old feeling came. It was insistent. He tried to extinguish the fire. Shifting, he tried to think the feeling away. No. No. Something in him wanted the scorching pleasure. His controlled burn went wild. More embarrassed than pleased, he barely enjoyed the release. He nearly collapsed on top of her.

She stopped kissing him. She placed her hands against his chest and pushed him back to sitting upright. "Stan…"

He wondered if she knew.

"I think we should slow down," she said. "I don't want…I think we should slow down."

He nodded. "We should."

They breathed heavily. The clock ticked in the kitchen. "Where are you going to stay?" she finally asked. "Do you have some place to stay?"

"I don't know," he said. "Could I sleep on your porch?" The cool wetness settled against his upper thigh. He couldn't believe what had happened.

"What?"

"Really, I don't mind."

She stood up. "I'll get you a blanket. You can sleep here on the couch." She left the room.

She returned with a pillow, too. He took the pillow and put it under his head. She draped the blanket over him.

"I'm so glad I came to you," he said. The pillow was cool against his face.

"I'm glad you're okay. I wasn't sure if you had drowned or what."

"I'm sorry, too," he said.

"Sorry?"

"Well, sorry about calling so late, and then coming here. It probably looks a little crazy."

She studied him. "It's okay," she said. "I've had my fair share of crazy. I'm used to it."

She wished him good night.

"You should know," he said after she'd stepped a few feet away, "what I see my new life being about. I mean, I can't go back. Not to the line. I can't do that kind of work again. I figured out that much while I was at the cabin."

"I know," she said.

"I'm afraid of making a mistake."

She walked back over to the couch. "Don't you think I'm scared, too? If I think about it too much, it's all a little eerie. Here with you, like this, at this time of night? I really don't know you at all. But, I like you. I liked you at the cabin. I could barely sleep after you called. I thought I'd made a mistake by not talking to you. I'm glad you came."

He didn't say anything. She walked again towards the darkness across the room. "Goodnight," she said.

Her door closed. He heard a lock being set. Then in a few seconds, unset. He felt the damp spot in his jeans touching against his thigh. He was sixteen again.

Chapter XIII

Pulled up from a thick mire, coming slowly into the levels of light, he rose to his name. "Stan? It's almost noon." He rubbed his eyes clear of crust and opened them. June stood near the couch in a business outfit almost identical to what she'd worn at the cabin except that it was peach. He stared at her, bleary eyed.

"Morning," he said.

"I woke up early," she smiled and shrugged. "I couldn't go back to sleep, so I went into work."

Stan mashed at his hair with his hands. He guessed that he looked pretty awful. "I could have slept forever."

"Did you want to keep sleeping?"

He shook his head. "No, I should get up."

"With hitting your head last night, I didn't think that you should sleep too long. How do you feel?"

He touched his forehead. "It only hurts now if I press on it," he said. "How does it look?" The shirt must have fallen off sometime in the night.

"It looks bad now," she said. "But maybe when you wash up it won't look so bad. Probably just bruised." She smiled quietly. "You had quite a night."

He nodded, sitting up and putting his feet on the floor. He looked under the couch.

"I washed the t-shirt. It's in the bathroom with some other clothes."

She pulled a curtain back. Sunlight flashed into the room. "I made some telephone calls today," she said.

"Yeah?" He stared at a square of light on the carpet.

"I think I'll be able to work it out with someone at the bank. I think I can buy you some time to sell your house."

He guessed he should have felt more grateful, more relieved, but he didn't feel much of anything. "That's great," he said. He looked at her and smiled.

"You do want to sell it, don't you?" she asked, studying his face.

"Of course I do. I've got no use for it."

She nodded. "Good. I didn't want to move too fast, but last night you sounded like you were pretty sure. I thought it was one of the reasons you came into town." She turned to the curtain and closed it again.

"I was sure," he said.

"Nothing is official yet. I made a few phone calls to see if there was anything that could be done. Like I said, the banks don't want to foreclose if they don't have to."

He nodded.

She left the room. She seemed nervous. He wondered if she had doubts, if maybe she didn't want him to leave. Why would she want him to stay? Who would want him to stay? "Hey, June?" he called.

"Yes," she said, stepping back into the room. She had a damp washcloth. Sitting next to him, she began to dab at his forehead. The white cloth turned pinkish. "The bruise doesn't even look too bad. Not yet, anyway," she said.

He took her hand and kissed it. Surely she was his saint.

"What, Stan?" She pulled the cloth away, squinted at his forehead, and then pressed the cloth to it again.

"I was going to ask you if you wanted to get some lunch."

"That'd be great," she said. "I'm starving."

He thought for a moment. "We'd need to drive to the cabin, though. When I got out of the river I...well, I just don't have my wallet with me."

She smiled. "I can treat," she said. "It's my turn. You treated last time out at the cabin."

He nodded. "That's right, you do owe me," he said, grinning.

They leaned forward and kissed.

She smiled at him. "The clothes are in the bathroom with a couple other things."

After his shower he found the clothes she'd left for him. Jeans, an oxford shirt, an old pair of tennis shoes and a sweater. He pulled Chris' band t-shirt on first. The pants were a little loose in the waist. Felt odd without underwear, but they were at least shorter than Dale's. The shirt and the sweater both had the initials V.S. on the tag. Old boyfriend? Fiancé? He felt as if he were wearing the clothing of a dead man. In a bag on the sink he found a razor, shaving cream, and a new toothbrush still in its packaging.

He lathered generously and then ran the blade into the thick beard. It caught and pulled, and he was bloody by the end. But, minus the nicks and gouges, he looked much more like the guy he'd been in Farmington Hills, the guy who shaved every morning so he could be smooth-faced for the grimy work on the line. His hair was still long. He pulled it back, found a rubber band, and wrenched it into a ponytail.

He pulled the bloodied bits of tissue from his face and went to find June.

"Wow," she said. "You look even better without the beard."

"Really?" He touched his smooth face.

Chapter XIV

The coffee pot was half full, its small orange light still on. He poured himself a cup, tasted it, and poured it down the drain. Burnt. He turned off the pot. Near it he found a note from June.

Stan— I woke up early and decided to go to work. I still need to make a few more calls about your house. I should be back before noon.   —June

He showered, put on the same jeans and t-shirt, the oxford. The shirt had been ironed. He hoped that they'd get out to the cabin to get some of his own clothes, his wallet. At least some underwear.

His mind went back to the day before.

Over lunch they'd decided to go horseback riding. His suggestion. Rachel always said he never wanted to do anything. Starting things off on the right foot with June. They needed to have a normal date.

Stan felt good being back in the woods. He was nervous about riding a horse and regretted suggesting it.

The man from the stable looked at him and smiled. "If you can sit in that saddle then you're all set. These horses know exactly what to do. They've walked these trails hundreds of times. And, Frankie's the best for a beginner—perfect for you. No surprises. Just does what he's supposed to do."

Out on the trail they passed some fenced-off fields, which soon became meadows, swaying with long grasses and trillium. The trail rose up a moraine. Stan picked out white birch, yellow birch, white pine, red pine, beech, sugar maple, and hemlock. Many of the leaves had already started the slow burn into color. Red, orange, yellow, gold. Birds flitted around in the branches. Clear signs marked the trail with silhouettes of horses and arrows burned into the wood. Stan breathed deeply of the forest air and felt at home.

One memory of the ride stayed with him. It might have been their first quarrel.

The trail had come to a fork. A sign indicated that the two-hour ride continued through the lowland, while a three-hour ride veered off up a slope.

"Let's go this way," he suggested. He tried to pull Frankie towards the new trail, but Frankie ignored his efforts.

She looked toward the three-hour trail. "I don't think we should. We didn't pay for that trip."

"We'll tell him we stopped for a while. Look, that trail heads up into better terrain. These trees are depressing." He pulled again at Frankie's reins. The horse stopped.

June stopped her horse. "Let's just keep going this way."

"Aren't you tired of this? We've been down in this marsh for at least a half hour."

"It'll get better. Plus, I think it's going to rain. I don't want to be stuck out on a longer trail if it does start raining. We'll just stay on the trail we paid for."

"Okay," he said, shrugging.

Now he wondered—*we'll just stay on the trail...?* True, she was paying for it. He guessed it was her call. Still her certainty, her finality troubled him. He shrugged. It had started raining. They would have got caught in it on the long trail. *We'll just stay on the trail.*

After riding, they'd come back to her house and ordered pizza. They talked. She had questions for him about his life. He answered. They made out for a while before turning in. The day had exhausted them both.

The pictures on June's walls weren't people from her life. Landscapes from department store art bins. Van Gogh's *Starry Night* hung over her bed.

He leaned against the opposite wall and studied the masterpiece. Nothing. He wanted to derive some kind of meaning from it. It was like staring at those Magic Eye stereograms that were a craze for a while. Management had hung one in the break room at the plant. For a time, the workers ignored it, speculating that it was some kind of ploy to get them to quit smoking or stop swearing. Then a few days later, someone said, "Holy shit, I see it! It's a fucking spaceship." Everyone gathered around squinting, closing one eye, staring blankly until they'd all seen it. Except for Stan. He'd told them he could see it, and he spent the next dozen breaks trying to see it, but nothing ever came in focus out of the mess of patterns and color. Eventually he started sitting on the other side of the break table.

It was the same with the Van Gogh. Stars too big to be stars, the swirling clouds, the craggy black tower. None of it made any sense. It looked like a kid's perspective. What made it a masterpiece? The price it fetched at auction?

He went through all the drawers in the kitchen, but finally had to get a light off of one of the gas burners. Holding his first drag, he stepped through a sliding glass door onto a small deck, and then exhaled. The nicotine filled his lungs like a willow root.

He wiped dead leaves and twigs from the chair on the deck. The glass top of the small table next to him was smeared with dust and dried rainwater. The deck looked out over a spacious backyard, partly overgrown lawn and partly neglected natural area filled with trees, English ivy, and maple seedlings, flanked by board fence. A thick woods grew at the back where the lawn ended. The grass needed mowing and it was infested by dandelions and weeds.

Birds flitted around an apple tree close to the deck. Two feeders hung from branches, both almost empty, but enough sunflower seeds in one to attract a blue jay, and enough thistle seed in the other to draw a few goldfinches.

The goldfinches flew back and forth between the thistle feeder and the higher branches of the tree. The jay fed from the sunflower seeds and the ground below. He squawked warnings at the smaller birds and sometimes chased them into other trees, though he never went after the thistle.

Stan thought of his sister. As a teenager, she'd made it her duty to keep the feeder in their yard full.

She always tried to do the right thing. She earned good grades, married a good man, gave their parents three good grandkids. In high school, she and Stan had fallen in with different crowds. Debbie was two years older and was off to Kalamazoo for college just when Stan earned his driver's license. Even then, she called every weekend, and always asked to talk to him first. He'd given her one-word answers to her questions.

He twisted his cigarette into the bottom of his shoe. Inside the house he found a portable phone and took it out to the deck. It would be good to call her. She'd be excited to hear about June. Maybe she'd get him excited again.

Stan didn't say anything right away, and his sister said "Hello?" again.

"So you probably didn't think it would be me, did you?"

"Stan?" Her voice was hesitant.

"Yup."

"God, I can't believe. Is something wrong?"

"Nothing's wrong. I just wanted to talk to you. I have something I want to tell you. Something I think you'll like."

"Okay."

"I met somebody." He felt his smile in his cheeks. The news would make her happy.

"What?" she asked excitedly.

"I said I met somebody."

"Really? That's great. Who is she? Where did you meet her?"

He cleared his throat. "I met her up at the cabin. She was walking in the woods, and she came out onto the property, and we got to talking and hit it off. Her name's June."

"At your cabin? That's great."

"Yeah, I've been heading up to the cabin quite a bit lately. It's a good place to clear my head." The jay flew down to the ground.

"That's great, Stan."

"Yeah, I'm at her place now in Gaylord. We went horseback riding yesterday." His sister would like to know these things. Ever since his loss, she had tried as best she could to get him to lead something like a normal life.

"Horseback riding. Sounds fun."

"It was okay. It rained."

She was quiet for a moment. "So, a long-distance relationship then?"

"Yeah, for now. It's working out so far," he said. "So, how are you and Mike?"

"Fine. Great. I'm keeping pretty busy with the kids. Mike was transferred into a different department. We didn't have to move this time, but he doesn't like the work as much. More contact with the customers. He likes it better behind the scenes."

"Yeah," Stan said. He tapped a cigarette out of the pack.

"But tell me more about June. What's she like?"

"She's a good person. She asks a lot of questions like she really wants to know about me. She's giving." He put the cigarette behind his ear.

"I like her already."

"She's good looking, probably out of my league, actually."

"Doesn't sound like she thinks so."

"Yeah. Don't tell her, okay?"

They laughed. Then they were quiet.

"I can't remember when you saw the kids last," Debbie said.

"Since the funeral, I guess," he said. He took the cigarette from behind his ear.

There was a prolonged silence. She sighed.

"Don't worry about it. I sure as hell haven't given you much reason to visit." The jay flew into the trees at the back of the yard and disappeared into the green.

"Well, you were in a bad way. I'm just so glad to hear about June and how things are going for you now."

He stood, slid the glass door back, and walked his cigarette over to the burner. He held the phone to his ear with his shoulder. "She's great," he said, talking around the cigarette.

"You're not really old, Stan. This could be a chance to start over, even have kids again. If you wanted to."

He took a drag. More kids? "I don't know," he exhaled. "I don't know about that right now. I don't know about anything." He took his cigarette back onto the deck. The blue jay hadn't returned.

"What's the matter?"

He sighed. "Maybe things are going fine," he said. "Hell, I don't know. I guess that's what scares me a little bit is I don't know anything." He took another drag.

"I would think you would be scared. Starting over, not knowing, can be scary. It's been awhile since you've tried to be with anyone."

He studied the growing ash of his cigarette. "It has. It scares the hell out of me."

"That sounds right to me. Relationships are scary. Wonderful, too."

"I don't know," he said.

"It sounds like you're looking for a reason not to start a relationship."

"I thought the same thing," he confessed. "But, I didn't run away. Still, I'm not sure I want to talk relationship, yet."

Debbie sighed. "You're talking yourself out of it right here on the phone. Have you said anything to her about this?"

"No, I haven't really—"

"Well, don't. You're going to ruin things before they even get started."

"But—"

"Shut up now and stop thinking so much. You're not at the altar. You're dating. Couldn't you just date and see where it goes?"

"I am."

"You'll regret this if you walk out now because you're a little scared."

"That makes sense," he said. "But I still wonder if I should be with anyone right now. It felt good to be alone, you know?"

Alone. He felt so natural sometimes. Like a fish in a river.

"You've *been* alone, though. For three years. Do you want to know how many times you've called me? *Not once.* Now you're seeing this woman, and you call me. I think she's taking you somewhere healthy. Out of your safety zone, but healthy." She always read lots of self-help books. Always ended up speaking the lingo. Safety zone. Boundaries. Inner child. He began to remember why he never called her.

He rubbed his eyes. "You're right. I know you're right, but I just can't get to feeling sure about this."

"Who is sure about anything? Do you think I'm sure all the time?"

"Nobody's sure, I guess," he said. "But I guess *I* want to be sure."

"Well, you can't be."

"It's hard to explain," he started. "It feels a little dangerous sometimes. I was thinking about it last night and couldn't sleep. I just don't want to get trapped."

"Dangerous? Trapped? What are you talking about now?"

"I've had a lot of time to think about things. I see things differently now."

"Like what? Differently, how? I'm not understanding this."

"Look," he said, "I haven't been totally honest with you." He took a breath. "Fact is, I quit my job. I've been living at the cabin."

"Oh God, Stan. Can you still get your job back?"

"I don't want it back. I figured that much out. I never want to work on the line again."

"What are you going to do, then?"

He sighed. "I don't know. But I don't want to happen what already happened to me." He touched the itchy bump on his forehead and then examined his fingers. No blood.

"Like what? What does that mean?"

"I don't think I did very much right. When I was young, I jumped after that job in the plant. I always thought that's what I wanted. Then I met Rachel. Jumped at that. Then we had Shannon. And then everything after that became things I had to do to keep things going. There wasn't much in it for me."

"You make your marriage sound pretty terrible," she said quietly. "I hope Mike doesn't think like that of us."

"He doesn't. He doesn't. Nobody thinks of it at the time, or at least not many people do. There's good times and there's bad times. That's expected. At the time, when they were alive and we were together, I just thought I was doing what everybody does. But then after they died, none of it made sense."

"None of what?"

"None of anything—my job, the house—any of it. There was nothing left to hold my life up. I was like a stranger to myself. And then up at the cabin I figured some things out. The whole time I was doing what I thought I was supposed to be doing, I wasn't. I just want a different life now, one that's more about me."

"And you don't want anybody in it with you?"

"I didn't say that. It's just that if I'm with someone, I want to feel like—I want to know—Oh, hell."

"What?"

"I'm not good at putting it into words. I don't even know if I know what I'm trying to put into words."

Debbie sighed. "So what are you going to do?"

"I don't know."

"Well, what do you want to do?"

"I don't *know!*" He closed his eyes and rubbed them with his fingers. "Wanting. It's not that simple."

Debbie was quiet, seeming to take everything in. "Sounds like what you want is a relationship that guarantees happiness, and you want a job that always means something to you, and you want a life that never has monotonous stretches? Am I right?

Because it sounds very reasonable, Stan."

He'd never won an argument with her. "Look," he said, "I should probably get off of June's phone. This is long distance."

"Okay. But promise me that you won't do anything stupid."

"Like what?" he asked.

"I don't know much about everything you've just been saying, but I think you have at least one thing going right for you with June. Take things slowly. Don't get married. Don't break up. In a couple months you can see where you are and see if you want to keep going. If not, then the two of you talk about it."

She was right. He pulled open the sliding door.

"With all that other stuff—" Debbie said. "It just sounds like you want too much. Life isn't like that. You don't get the gold ring every time. I don't know that you'll find what you're looking for. I hope it doesn't keep you from finding what you can have."

"Okay, okay," he said. He felt tired.

They said they loved each other. Then he hung up.

A moment later, the phone rang. Was she calling back? Maybe she had caller ID. The phone rang a second time. He decided that if it was her, he didn't want to talk anymore.

The answering machine beeped, and June's voice invited the caller to leave a message. A man spoke: "Hi, June. I wanted you to know that you're dad invited me to the party tonight. I'm going to be there. I have to be, really. I didn't want you to think that I asked to be there. I would like to talk to you. I could even take you to a movie." He forced a laugh. "But don't think that I came to bother you. When the boss asks, you go to the boss's party. Right? Anyway, when you see me there you can talk to me if you want. Or not. Bye."

Rubbing his lower lip between his thumb and finger, Stan thought about the message. Ex-fiancé? She hadn't mentioned that her ex worked for her dad. She hadn't even mentioned that her dad had a business. How much did he really know about her? She was the one always asking the questions. Who was this guy? The message gnawed at him. He felt the burn of jealousy for the first time since high school.

He went into the living room to wait for her on the couch. He thought about turning the television on, but decided against it. After a few minutes, he lay down.

Chapter XV

Metal clinked against metal. A drawer slid slowly open. Stan opened his eyes. He was on the couch, and the noises were coming from the kitchen. June—trying to take out pots and pans as quietly as she could. He listened for a minute.

"June?"

She came into the living room and apologized for waking him. She was wearing a t-shirt and jeans. He liked the look on her. His sister was right. He shouldn't screw this up.

"You look really good," he said.

She blushed and then thanked him. "I made an appointment for Monday about your house."

He nodded. "You have a message you might want to listen to."

She looked at the blinking light on the answering machine, and then walked over to it. "Who is it from?"

He shrugged. Then he sat up. "Some guy."

"A guy?" She pressed the button and listened to the message. Half way through, she started to shake her head.

"So who's that?" he asked.

"Nobody."

"It doesn't sound like nobody." He pressed his back into the couch. "Sounds like a somebody. Sounds like a somebody that wants to see you." He tried to find a happy medium between teasing and accusation.

"He might, but I don't want to see him."

"Sounds like there might be some history there."

"Stan."

"What?"

"I don't have anything going on."

"So who was that?"

"His name is Alan Marsh. I've known him since high school. He works for my dad. He's started asking me out recently. He's nobody. I've told him no every time he's asked me out. I don't like him."

"Okay," he said. "I just wanted to know." They grew quiet. Something came to him. "What day is it today?"

"What?"

"Seriously. I really don't know."

"It's Friday."

He looked into her eyes and smiled.

"What?"

"Let's go to the cabin," he said. "We could take some steaks. I know I have tomatoes that are almost ripe. After dinner, we could sit out on the porch, have some wine, see where things go." He smiled again. His blood raced with the idea of it. "We could redo the other day, but do it right."

She shook her head. "I can't."

"What? Why? Do you have to work this afternoon? We could wait until you're done. I could go shopping, and then when you get back we could drive out there." It was what they needed to do. Despite his mixed feelings, he needed to try to make things work with her. It felt right to go to the cabin again and start over.

Shaking her head, she stood up. "It's not work," she said. "There's a birthday party for my father. He's turning seventy-five. I have to go."

A heaviness settled over Stan. He felt instantly tired. "That's the party that Alan guy was talking about?"

She nodded.

"And you have to go?"

"It's my dad."

"How late does the party go?"

"I don't know," she said. "I was hoping we'd find out together. I called my dad already and told him I was bringing someone."

"You did?" She wanted him to meet the old man?

"I hope it's okay."

"Your dad's birthday?" He imagined gathering around a table with a bunch of smiling strangers to sing "Happy Birthday" to an old man. The old man would smile at everyone except for Stan. For him he'd reserve a cautious frown. "I really doubt your dad wants some guy he doesn't know at his party."

"I already talked to him. It's fine. He wants to meet you."

"What did you tell him about me?"

She sat down on the couch. "I couldn't really tell him all of it. I said I met you a couple weeks ago. I told him about the cabin, though."

"*What* about the cabin?"

"Just that you have a cabin up here."

"Did you tell him I don't have a job? He must have loved that."

"I said that you were laid off and that you were up at your cabin trying to figure out if you really wanted to spend the rest of your life on the line. I told him that you were looking to relocate and start over." She rubbed her hand on his back. "I told him about your wife and daughter, too."

"Why did you have to tell him that?" Even as he questioned her, a part of him already knew. "Oh, I get it. I can almost hear your father's voice on the telephone: 'Are you sure this is the kind of guy you want to get involved with? Laid off. Not sure what he wants to do with his life. Living alone in some goddamn shack. Most guys have a little more stability by his age. I just don't think—' And then you sprung it. Dad didn't even see it coming. A sucker punch. What could he do besides back peddle? How do you criticize someone's lack of stability after you hear something like that? Losing your wife and child in a car accident. Of course, you had to tell him. It was your trump card."

"I'm not that devious. When you know me better, you'll know."

He put his hand over both of hers. "It's okay. I'm sorry I made it sound that way. It's not like it's not the truth. I'm not used to this. I'm going to say stupid things." But even as he consoled her, he resented the deaths of his wife and child being used to win an argument. Whether she admitted it or not, he was right. "I still don't know about this party, though. I don't feel ready for something like that. Couldn't you make up some reason why I couldn't make it?"

She didn't say anything, but just looked at his face. Her own face changed as though she'd seen something in his that bothered her. She got up and left the room.

He hoped she wasn't fed up with him. "June?" Sitting on the edge of the couch, he recalled all the times Rachel had stormed out of the room in frustration. His stubbornness had been the cause of more than one fight.

"Look," she said, coming back into the room. "I understand that you don't really want to go to my father's. I don't blame you. It's too soon. But I talked to him today on the phone. I was so happy about you being here, and it just came up. I can tell him you couldn't make it. I can tell him anything. But I'd like it if you came with me."

"I'll go," he said.

She sat next to him on the couch. "You don't have to. I understand—"

"No," he continued. "I want to go." He doubted the words as he said them, but they seemed like the words he should be saying.

"I can't promise you it will be fun. It might be really boring."

"It will be fun if you're there," he said. He reached up and brushed her bang from her eyes. He felt like he was reading a script, maybe the right script this time. "But tomorrow," he continued, "we have to go out to the cabin. I don't want you to have rotten memories of the place. We'll start over. Catch a few fish. Eat corn. Whatever else." He smiled.

Nodding, she leaned towards him and they kissed.

He pulled out of their embrace. "That guy from the answering machine is going to be there tonight. I'll have to meet him."

"It sounds like it," she said. "I'm sorry."

"Great."

She put her hands over his. "It won't be bad. Alan…well, Alan isn't much."

"You don't have *any* feelings for him?" He searched her eyes. Something about this—the unrequited lover. His tinges of jealousy made him feel that there was more to what he had with June.

She shook her head. They kissed again for awhile. Her lips were soft.

"Let me make you some breakfast," she said. "Or, I guess brunch."

Chapter XVI

He wanted to begin to explain what he thought his time at the cabin had taught him. The taste of the breakfast she'd made was still in his mouth—eggs, the salty sausage. He took a drink from his coffee. "See, now that I'm trying…I knew this wouldn't be easy."

"Well, you don't have to talk about it right now," she said. "Wait till you're ready."

"No, I want to try." He cleared his throat. "What I think now is that nobody is doing what they're supposed to be doing. Or, not many people are. I think we end up in places that we shouldn't be, but by the time we get there it's too late to do much about it. Or more likely we don't even realize we're there. I'm a perfect example."

She looked at him, her eyebrows going up encouragingly.

"Look at my life. I—"

"What *about* your life?" she asked. "You had a good job. You had a wife and child. You had a home and a vacation place. Unless there's something you're not telling me."

He nodded. "Yes, of course, I see all that. But look at it now. I've got nothing."

"Nothing?" she asked. She touched her coffee cup with the fingertips of both hands.

"I know I'm starting to get something back now, but for years I had nothing." He stood, walked over to the sink, and poured the rest of his coffee down the drain. "Without Rachel and Shannon, it's like my life vanished."

"I'm not sure how this is an example of what you were talking about. You were talking about how everyone— I mean, you were saying *we*, like people in general. Not everyone loses— Not everyone goes through what you went through."

He leaned against the counter. He sighed. "I think I'm here now because I never learned who I was. I didn't know anything and I was making some of the biggest decisions of my life in complete ignorance. And, everyone around me was smiling and nodding and throwing rice like everything I was doing was good. Was right."

"What wasn't good?"

"I can't say exactly that anything wasn't good, but it wasn't right. What would have been right would have been for me to take some time to know something."

"Stan, I don't— Tell me what was bad exactly. What aren't you telling me?"

"Nothing. Nothing was bad. Rachel wasn't. We had our problems, sure. But, I don't think we were any worse off than others, which I guess is my point. And Shannon was great. But now they're both gone, and I don't— I shouldn't be like this."

June folded a leg up under her. "Like what?"

"Do you want to sit outside?" he asked, stalling.

Stan pulled the door back. Birds whistled. "I was out here earlier," he said. "You've got a nice view."

She followed him, but he could tell that she didn't want the conversation. He couldn't really blame her. He was no good with words.

She sat at the table. He pushed himself up onto the railing of the deck. It creaked under him. He looked out towards the stand of trees at the end of the yard.

"I don't want you to be afraid of anything I'm trying to say," he said. He turned and looked into her face.

"I'm not afraid," she said. "A little confused, but not scared. Besides, there's no river for me to dive in and swim away. So you have nothing to worry about."

He smiled weakly. "Well, I didn't mean afraid, exactly. I just meant that I don't want you to be bothered by it. I don't want you to think that I'm some kind of nut. I feel like I can say these things to you. I need to."

He looked at the tree. "I think there's something wrong because nothing I did was for me. I mean, look, my wife and child die, and I can't give one reason for anything. Why do I work where I work? Why do I own a house? Why, for three years, do I do nothing except go to work and earn money to pay for the things that no longer mean anything to me? Three years. Doesn't it seem strange?" He looked at her, waiting.

She shrugged. "You had an incredible loss. Nobody could say that anything you went through was strange. Everyone mourns differently."

He nodded. "That makes sense if it was just mourning. But, eventually I started to feel okay with what had happened. I mean, I'm sure I'll always be mourning in some way. But I'm seeing now that there's something else that I lost that I didn't know about until I lost Rachel and Shannon. I had lost myself."

"Aren't you starting to come back now? Aren't you finding things? I know I am."

She'd had her own loss. She had an ex-fiancé. That was a story he hadn't even asked about. Whatever the details, they'd scarred her. "Sure I'm starting to feel things...with you. I mean, it's good. But I'm cautious."

"I'm cautious, too. We have to be. But, not so cautious that we keep good things from happening."

He looked at the deck. "I don't think I'm cautious the way you mean. It's not that I'm afraid of being hurt. I don't want to lose myself again."

She stood up. "Stan. What are you trying to tell me?"

He looked at her. Something in her face told him that she was taking this conversation the wrong way. "I'm trying to tell you what I think I figured out, or at least what I think I need to figure out."

"Well, if that's it, then okay. But if it's something else, I need you to be honest." She sat again.

He scratched his ear. "I'm going to start again, okay?"

She nodded.

"I think many people end up like me except they don't know it. Stuck in jobs. I don't think many people are doing something that means anything to them. Forty, fifty, sixty hours a week—just for money. That was me. I didn't hate it, but I was numb. Numb."

She looked down.

"I think that most people are numb. Think about your own

job," he started. "Does it mean anything to you?"

"Yes, it does."

He looked at her doubtfully. "But, really though. What you do means something to you, and you think it's a part of who you are?"

She crossed her arms over her chest. "I don't know about that. But yes, it means something to me."

"What does it mean to you?"

"It's a good job, and I do it well. I'm proud of what I do."

"Why?"

"What?"

"Why are you proud of what you do?"

"I went to school for it, and I'm good at it. It's a good job. Mostly I make profits for some big bank in Detroit, but along the way I can help people, get them out of jams. Like you. Get their lives back on track after they've been sick or done something foolish. Or a death or divorce. A lot of people just run into the ditch financially. And I help."

"Would you do it if they didn't pay you to do it?"

She looked at the table, and then answered after a moment. "No, I guess I wouldn't. But I don't see where—" She looked up from the table. "You make sacrifices to have other things. Compromises. What do you expect life to be? If they could get people to work for the fun of it, they wouldn't bother paying. Every job has to be a *little* tiresome. If it was like going to Disneyland, I'd have to pay *them*."

"I don't want to seem impossible. I guess I just think that the sacrifices shouldn't include sacrificing myself. I understand that you have to give up things to have things. And family comes with its own rewards. I had good times with Rachel and Shannon. I did. But now they're gone, and I see that I was just playing a part doing everything I thought I should be doing, making *sacrifices*—big ones—"

June sighed. "So, then what do you want to do? What do you expect?"

He set his face in his hands and rubbed his fingers into his forehead. "I don't know. I haven't figured that part out yet."

"Do you have to find out alone? Did you figure out that you're happiest when you have nobody in your life? Is that what you want to tell me?"

He looked up. He sighed. "No. I was really lonely sometimes at the cabin. I do need people, I know that."

She stood up and walked towards him. She put her arms around him and set her head against his chest. "Can you let someone be a part of it as you figure it out?"

He put his arms around her. It felt good. "Yes. Of course." He shook his head. Why couldn't he explain it better?

They held each other for a time. He looked out over her head towards the long, wild grass of the backyard. "Do you have a lawn mower?" he asked.

"What?"

"I want to knock out the backyard for you. If somebody doesn't do something soon, it's going to get too long to cut."

She told him that there was a mower in the garage.

He pulled the cord until his arm grew tired. The sun was high in the west, but not hot. Finally, after changing the spark plug, he was able to get the little engine to cough to life. The mowing went well around the edges where there were patches of yellowed or dead grass. The lawn collapsed in neat rows. Other things needed to be done. Weeding the flowerbed, pruning the bushes, cutting back branches. The yard was a jungle of neglect. There was at least a weekend's worth of work.

Nearer the center of the yard, where the lawn was thickest, the little engine struggled and stalled. He turned it on its side several times and cleared the grass underneath. He could only push the mower a few feet before it would clog and stall again. He swore at the mower, at the grass, at everything.

"Stan," June called from a window, "you'll probably want to come in soon and get ready."

Leaving the square of lawn unfinished, he left the mower where it died and went back to the house.

Chapter XVII

Stan asked to drive. He followed the main drag of Gaylord for a few miles and then June had him turn north onto a cracked, gray secondary road. Weathered mailboxes teetered at the edges. The homes didn't look in much better shape. Nearly every one had at least one car or truck rusting in the front yard, grass growing tall around it.

"Your dad doesn't live in town?"

"He likes it out here."

He imagined the man living in one of these run-down houses. Then he remembered that her dad owned a business. Probably pretty well off. At least he lived out in the country. Probably knew something about simplicity. The grass around his place would be long, wild. Her dad would have spent winters surrounded by acres of cold white. Maybe he'd be down-to-earth. Maybe he'd be open to the new guy in her life, the out-of-work factory rat who doesn't know who he is or what he wants to do. Stan eased back into his seat and enjoyed the drive.

"It's beautiful, isn't it?" he said.

"What?"

"The colors."

"Green?"

"It's more than just green," he explained. "If you look, it's every shade of green."

June looked out her window. "I guess it's pretty," she said. "It's different when you grow up here."

She turned on the radio. A country song was playing. "Do you like country?" she asked. "That's my favorite."

"Johnny Cash."

She laughed. "I like newer artists."

June undid her belt, slid next to him, and put her arm around his neck. Her other hand rested on his thigh. She sang along softly with the song on the radio. It was something about finding love. Or losing love. One or the other.

Driving this way, not talking about anything too heavy, the warmth of a woman's arm around him, he couldn't remember when he'd felt so good. He set his hand on her hand. They didn't move. Songs of love and loss came one after the other.

"It's up here," she said.

Ahead, on either side of the road, dozens of cars were parked.

"Popular guy," he said.

"He knows lots of people. He's done a lot for the town."

Through the trees, flashes of the house came. There was nothing down-to-earth about it. "Damn, it's a mansion!" Stan exclaimed. "Where are we? Fort Michilimackinac?"

June told him about the house as they walked. Based on Adirondack style, three stories, five bedrooms, three full bathrooms, a Jacuzzi. Thousand-square-foot great room. Three fire places, a smaller living room, a library, and a two-story deck that wrapped around the back and one side of the house. Either staircase of the deck walked down to two acres of lawn. Among other things, it also had a small screening room. "Like a little movie theater. He owns a few movie theaters."

Most of the people were on the deck with drinks. They were dressed casually, but only Stan wore jeans. Everyone said hello to June as they walked past. Some of them turned odd looks on Stan. They whispered to each other and motioned towards him with their chins. "There's a resemblance," he heard one woman say. "You think so?" asked another.

June tried to find her father. "He's around here somewhere," she said.

"It's a big place," he said. "Easy to get lost."

She smiled and nodded. "Maybe if we stay still, he'll find us." Resting their elbows on it, they leaned against the railing of the upper deck.

The house on the hill. Red and jack pines rose up on hills upon hills into the distance. "It's a great view," he said. She held his hand, and he liked the feeling of her fingers braided into his. He hadn't guessed that he would feel so good. The next day they would be at the cabin together. He felt even better.

She asked if he wanted something to drink. "I'm sure he has whiskey."

"Just a beer would be fine, I think. I see some people are drinking beer."

She started to leave, stared into the people around them, and then leaned next to him again. "Alan Marsh is coming over here," she whispered. "The guy on the phone. You'll see what I mean."

"Hi, June," Alan said, arriving through the people.

Alan had acne. Dark bags swelled under his eyes. He was taller than Stan, but slight.

"Have you seen my dad?" June asked.

"Not in a while," he said. "I saw him inside when I came in, but that was over an hour ago. When did *you* get here? How are you?" He tilted his beer and finished what was left, taking a quick sidelong glance at Stan.

"We just got here. But where are my manners? Alan, this is Stan Carter," she said. "Stan, Alan Marsh. Works for Daddy."

Stan held out his hand, and Alan grabbed it. His grip was cold and wet.

"Sam?" he asked.

Something seemed strange about Alan. Either there was something wrong with his wiring or he'd had a lot of beer. "Stan," he corrected.

Alan nodded and then dropped Stan's hand. He turned back to June, physically excluding Stan from the conversation. "So, how *are* you?"

"I've been fine. Really busy with work. Some investment things for Stan." She kissed Stan on the cheek, turning her back on Alan. Stan thought, *It's like a dance.*

"Well, like I said, I didn't come over to— I just wanted, or thought, that I should say hello."

"Uh huh," June said.

He looked at Stan one last time, took his full measure, and walked away.

"He's a charmer," Stan said.

"He's just been drinking." She watched Alan walk away. "Sometimes I feel sorry for him."

Alan threaded his way across the deck and disappeared down the stairs.

"I hope my dad doesn't find out that Alan's had so much to drink. He doesn't go for that kind of thing at one of his parties, especially with an employee." She shook her head.

"What does he do for your dad?"

"He's an assistant manager. Dad doesn't really like him, but Alan's been with the theater since he was sixteen. He went from usher to projectionist and then to assistant manager. Dad said he'll never make him a manager, though."

"Why?"

"Just doesn't trust him. Something about Alan bothers him. I don't see it, but he says Alan has a dark side."

"And you never dated him?" he asked. "Because you talk like you know a lot about him. You talk like you even care about him."

She leaned close to him and looked out towards the trees. "I've known Alan since high school. He's liked me for a long time. I never liked him. I know a lot about a lot of my dad's employees. I guess Dad's a gossip. No, I never dated Alan Marsh. And it's not because he didn't ask me."

He took her hand again. They looked at the trees.

"Do you still want a beer?"

He nodded and she said that she'd be right back. For a moment, until she disappeared into the people, he enjoyed watching her walk away. He felt lucky. Then he turned back to the trees. Marking them, he watched their shadows grow slowly across the lawn.

"Managing to get through this with a smile?" a voice asked from behind him.

Stan turned around. A compact man smaller than Stan, but heavier, extended his hand and introduced himself. "Pete. June's older brother. June told me to come over and introduce myself. You met the old man, yet?"

"Stan. I guess you knew that. Haven't met your dad yet." Most of Pete's blondish hair wrapped around the sides and back of his head. The only thing that kept him from looking like every other bald guy was a tuft of thick hair above his forehead, the last remnant of a widow's peak.

"No wonder you're still smiling." Pete took a drink.

"What do you mean? Is he that bad?"

Pete laughed. "No, not really. If you're his son, maybe. Kind of an old lion. But you're with June, so maybe he won't eat you alive."

In the distance, over Pete's shoulder, Alan Marsh stood at the top of the stairs studying him. He took a pull from his beer and disappeared down to the lower level again.

"You're really making me want to meet him," Stan said, smiling.

Pete laughed again. "I didn't mean to make him out so bad. Just something to say. You know, the girlfriend's old man and all that."

Stan's mind caught on the word *girlfriend*.

"So, where was June off to, anyway?" Pete asked.

"She went to get me something to drink."

"Like what," Pete asked, grinning. "A nice, tall glass of water?"

"Sure," he said, laughing. He liked Pete already.

"Dad told me June was bringing someone tonight. How long have you two been seeing each other?" He took another drink.

Stan tried to remember the amount of time she'd made up. "A while, now."

Pete nodded and looked out toward the backyard.

"How far does your dad's property go back? Does it stop at the tree line?"

Pete shook his head. "No, it goes back another couple acres into the woods," he said, waving his hand toward the trees. "There's a creek back there, and his property ends just after the creek."

"A creek?" Stan asked. "What creek? Any trout in it?" The thought of moving water excited him.

Pete shook his head. "I don't know the name...or anything really. The old man just said there's a creek back there."

Stan nodded. "So, do you live in the area?"

Pete smiled broadly, nodding. "Been in Gaylord all my life. I manage two of my dad's theaters."

"I guess I'm probably moving to this area, too," Stan said.

"Really?" He asked Stan where he lived.

He told him about the engine assembly plant in Novi.

Pete finished his drink. "What are you going to do up here?"

He shrugged.

Pete looked at him.

"It was time for me to get off the line," he explained. "When it's time, it's time. I have a little cabin over on the Black River. I've been staying there. I haven't really started the job hunt. I'll start looking come Monday."

Pete still looked at him. "Hey, I don't want to be a bummer, but unemployment's pretty high around here. Just be ready to look for a while."

He nodded. "I have a little money saved. And, I don't need much, really."

Pete looked at him again, nodded, and then looked away. "I hope you're not thirsty." He motioned toward a picture window.

Following Pete's gesture, Stan saw June talking with an older woman. The woman squeezed June's shoulder and nodded. June didn't have a beer in her hand. Stan shrugged. He tried to see the creek through the trees.

A small boy, maybe five or six, ran up and hugged Pete's leg. "Daddy, Mommy wants you to come down."

Pete smiled at Stan. "Tell her I'll be right there."

"She said *now*." The boy ran into the clutch of adults.

"Gosh, Petey," a gray haired man shouted, "it seems like you were that small only yesterday. And you had more hair."

Pete laughed. "Yeah, I bet" he shouted back. He looked at Stan. "Should I tell him that it seems like he should have been dead a long time ago," he whispered.

Stan laughed.

Pete offered his hand again. "Well, hey, I'll talk to you later, I'm sure."

"Good to meet you," he said, and meant it.

110

Pete moved slowly through the people. Many stopped him and shook his hand. One rumpled his tuft and then held a hand at knee-level. Stan guessed that he was indicating how small he had been only yesterday. He watched Pete until he finally made it to the stairs. Alan Marsh was standing there again. Another man, thicker in build, was standing with him. They both nodded to Pete as he went by. When they saw Stan looking their way, they went down the stairs. He shook his head. *What the hell? High school games.*

He turned back to the trees, which had grown darker. Above them the setting sun still shone brightly. If he went soon, he could get back to the woods and to the creek. He knew the water the way he would never know people, the urgency of the little current. He knew its sound, where it was coming from, where it was going. Through the window, June was still talking to the woman. Probably wouldn't even know he was gone.

Unlike Pete, he made his way easily across the deck, down both flights of stairs, and then onto the lawn. Nobody tried to talk to him. He didn't plan to stay at the creek long. He just wanted to see it. He started across the grass. It was perfect. Not a weed to be found.

"Hey?"

Stan recognized Alan Marsh's voice. He wasn't really surprised. He turned around.

"Where you going?" Alan challenged, lifting his chin. His eyes were unsteady.

Stan looked at him for a moment. "Pete said there's a creek back in the woods. I just thought I'd—"

"Pete," Alan barked. "You mean Mr. Thorpe, don't you?" He stepped awkwardly to his left and then caught himself and regained his balance. "He's never told me to call him Pete. I've known him a helluva lot longer than you."

Stan looked at him. "Look, I don't have a lot of light. I just want to get back—"

"So, who the fuck are you all of the sudden?" Alan stepped forward.

Stan looked him up and down. "What?"

Alan's sneer softened. "I just don't get it. One day June's not seeing anybody, and the next you show up at her dad's party." He waved his hand.

"I'm not sure what there is to *get*." The long shadows of the pines covered the lawn. It would be too dark soon to see anything. He started to turn.

Alan grabbed his arm. "Look, I've put in a lot...I've been waiting for things to fall apart between her and Vince. I saw it coming. I don't think you should be here, in the way."

He wrenched his arm free of Alan's grip. Something about the name Vince caught in his mind like a burr. "What do you want from me?" he said.

"Stop seeing her." He pointed at Stan. "You're fucking things up."

"Isn't that up to her?" He took a step towards Alan, who almost fell over in his effort to take a few steps back.

Behind Alan, an old barrel-chested man stepped off the stairs and started across the lawn towards them with his shoulders back. *Like one of those arctic ice breakers*, Stan thought. He seemed to be watching.

Alan clenched his fists and stared.

Stan snickered. "You aren't going to do shit," he said. "Go sleep it off." His heart banged against his ribs, anxious for something to happen. Alan seemed like a bluffer, but still. The old man was nearing them.

Alan looked Stan in the face one more time and then turned around. When he was only inches from the old man, he seemed to notice him and looked up.

"Alan?" the old man asked. "What's the—"

Stan didn't stay to hear the rest. The adrenaline began to ooze away and left him feeling sick. Still, he wanted to try to make it to the creek. Nearly to the end of the lawn and the beginning of the woods, he heard someone call his name. The old man.

Stan turned around. Probably June's dad.

"You're not running out, are you?" He laughed. "Not another

one." When he was about five feet from Stan, he extended his hand. "I'm June's father." He looked at Stan's ponytail.

Stan grasped the old man's dry palm. "No. Not running out. Your son told me that there's a creek back in the woods. I wanted to take a look at it." His first impulse was to lie, but he couldn't think of another reason for his walk in the woods. A cool breeze blew across the yard and chilled him. He shook the old man's hand more. "It's good to meet you."

Mr. Thorpe looked at him and his brows furrowed. He shook his head. "The creek's nothing to look at. It's just a little piss stream of a thing," he said.

Stan nodded.

"I'm Pete," the old man said. "Pete Senior. June told me that you two have been seeing each other for a while."

"A while," he said.

"Well, come on back to the house with me. Let's talk." He smiled. Stan reminded himself, *Old lion.*

Chapter XVIII

The house glowed from within and from the decks. Ephorons swarmed around the floodlights. Had they hatched off the creek? Looking back towards the trees, Stan was surprised by how dark they'd grown. He didn't say anything as they walked across the lawn. Neither did Mr. Thorpe. Pete Senior. Stan felt he needed to say something. He decided that he'd tell him how much he admired his property, but by then they were back to the house. Guests of the party began to stop Mr. Thorpe to wish him a happy birthday. He was cordial, but brief. The well-wishers talked for a moment, looked curiously at Stan, and then stepped away.

"Dad," June said from behind them.

Stan and Mr. Thorpe turned around.

"So, you two met." She was smiling. She hugged her father. "Happy birthday."

"Yeah," he said. "I caught him running off into the woods."

Stan's forehead tingled.

June looked a little startled. "What?"

Her father laughed. "Ah come on, don't worry. He was just out by the woods. He was…he was…What were you doing back there?"

Stan looked at June. "Your brother said there was a creek back there. I was just going back to look at it when your dad stopped me."

"You met Petey, then? Good. How'd you'd get along?"

"I liked him. It wasn't for long. His little boy came and pulled him away."

She nodded, smiling. "That would be Pete number three."

"We're just going into the den," her father said, turning to June. "To talk."

She looked at her father and smiled knowingly. She put something cold in Stan's hand. "Your beer," she said. She kissed his cheek.

What did he and Mr. Thorpe have to talk about?

In the house, Mr. Thorpe was stopped again and again, distributed smiles, kisses, handshakes. Stan took sips from his beer and waited, stepping forward to shake hands as Mr. Thorpe introduced him to strangers, smiled at their jokes, raised his beer in salute.

The old man opened a door and motioned for Stan to go in first. The den was nearly as big as his entire cabin. It smelled of leather. A pool table took up most of the middle of the room. Bookcases lined the walls with golf trophies and community awards occupying most of the space usually reserved for books. Two leather chairs positioned so perfectly in front of the fireplace they looked like they were already engaged in conversation. Mr. Thorpe walked past them. Stan followed. At the far end of the room, he saw a desk with two chairs in front of it. Mr. Thorpe motioned for him to take a seat in one of the chairs. Then, he made his way around the desk, pulled out its chair, and sat down.

It reminded Stan of an interview.

"How's your beer? Need another?" Mr. Thorpe asked.

The bottle in Stan's hand was empty. Maybe the old man was testing to see how much of a drinker he was. "No," he said. "I'm okay."

Mr. Thorpe nodded. He asked what Stan and Alan had been talking about.

Stan raised his eyebrows. "Hmm?"

"Out on the lawn. Alan was talking with you. He looked upset about something when he went past me." The old man leaned back into his chair, smoothing his hands over his thick white hair.

"We didn't say much, really," Stan started. "He just...well, he just thought I looked familiar like somebody he might have known."

"Must have upset him to find out that you weren't who he guessed."

"I wouldn't know why he looked upset."

The old man shrugged. "He's always been a moody little cuss. If I'd had any reason to I'd have fired him a long time ago." He sat forward and rested his palms on the desk.

Stan didn't say anything. For the first time he felt a little sorry for Alan. He could see clearly how he'd put everything he had into the job and into the idea of being with June. It was sad. The murmur of the party hummed from behind the closed door. Mr. Thorpe seemed to be waiting for him to speak. "Beautiful house," Stan offered, "The property and the decks. All of it."

Mr. Thorpe thanked him. "It's a nice little place," he said, smiling.

"June said you have a theater in the house. Do you watch a lot of movies?" Stan rubbed an itch out of his eyes.

Mr. Thorpe laughed. "Hell, no. You know, I really can't stand movies. My wife liked them. Especially the old ones. When we planned the house, it was her idea to have the theater."

"You don't like movies?"

Mr. Thorpe exhaled a short laugh through his nose. "Nope, not really." Then he was quiet again. He studied Stan for a moment before walking over to a small liquor cabinet. "Have a brandy with me?"

"Sure." The old man's back moved as he took out the glasses and poured. "How did you get into the theater business?" Stan asked, feeling compelled to fill the silences.

Mr. Thorpe turned around and walked the drink to him. Snifters. Then he took his own and sat down again. "I saw an opportunity," he said. "I was twenty years old. On a trip to Detroit with my parents, I saw my first movie. *Pitfall.* I remember that Raymond Burr was in it. I really don't recall much else except the packed theater. Every seat was taken. And they were all chewing on popcorn and sucking on fountain drinks." He stopped and took a sip of his drink. "It's a beautiful sound." He smiled.

Stan inhaled from the bowl of his snifter and took a sip of the brandy. "Smooth."

"When I got back to Gaylord," Mr. Thorpe continued, "I was able to convince a few men to back me financially. Keep in mind that I was twenty years old at the time. But I knew that's what Gaylord needed. A movie theater. And, they could see that I had something. For the first year, I didn't hire anybody. I sold tickets, worked the concession, and then ran the pictures. I taught myself how to run the projectors. In five years I had paid off those who had backed me. With interest. Five years after that I put a theater in Grayling. In '62 I built a theater in Cadillac. Seventy-three I put a second theater in Gaylord. In '75 I bought the theaters that were already in Alpena and Rogers City. From there it's pretty much been a gold mine. Up here I don't have to compete with the multiplexes. Some people have even complained in the local newspapers that I have a monopoly, but I've never done anything to keep someone from building a theater to compete with me." He smiled.

Stan scratched his head. "That's a great story. I mean, *it* could be a movie. It's amazing that at twenty years old you knew exactly what you wanted to do."

"Well," Mr. Thorpe said, "I knew I wanted to make money. Watching my parents, I'd already seen what not having money was like. In fact, do you know why I was in Detroit in '48?"

The old man seemed to be waiting for a response. Stan shook his head. "Why?"

"My dad had to go to Detroit to ask my mother's brother for a loan. Dad didn't have enough to get us through the winter. Can you imagine heading into a Michigan winter, and you don't have the money it will take to heat a house or fill a refrigerator?"

Imagining it, Stan shook his head. "Was your dad out of work?"

"He may as well have been. Do you know what he did?" Mr. Thorpe lay his palms flat on the desk.

Again, Stan felt obliged to shake his head.

"He carved wood."

Stan raised his eyebrows.

Mr. Thorpe nodded his head and laughed. "That's what he did. He had a little workshop and he carved. When he'd carved enough pieces, he took them down to Detroit or Flint and sold them at fairs. He did okay with walking sticks, especially canes, but he hated carving them. So instead he did things like this." He picked a piece of wood up from his desk. It had been carved into an exact replica of an open rose.

"It's beautiful," Stan said. "Things like that didn't sell?"

Mr. Thorpe shook his head. "In wood carving, people seemed to like big things or at least they'd pay more for them. Dad would put hours into these intricate pieces, but nobody ever wanted to pay what he asked for them. Customers haggled him down so he had to take next to nothing for the time he'd put in."

Stan listened. Above him it sounded like someone was drumming fingers on one of the ceiling tiles. He heard it again. Probably a mouse.

"It was his own fault, though," Mr. Thorpe continued. "At one point he started getting into carving and painting duck decoys. Jesus, he was good. Too good. He'd spend all summer and get seven or eight ducks finished. Like they were art or something. But hunters just wanted decoys. To hunt with. They didn't want to pay dad for what his job was really worth, and he couldn't afford to refuse whatever they offered." He shook his head. "And, nobody told him he had to make wood carving his main source of income. He'd always whittled, but he had a good job in a lumber mill too. Then, when I turned fifteen, he quit the mill and started carving full time. Wasn't long after that when my mom had to go to work at a grocery."

"Was he ever able to make the wood carving profitable?"

"Not really. In '49, he went back to the mill. Mom died of pneumonia in '53. Wasn't long after that all the mills started cutting back jobs. Dad was let go in '55. By then, though, I needed help with the theater, so I trained him to run the projectors. Eventually, he managed the Grayling theater for me, until about '70 when I helped him retire down to Florida."

Stan nodded. "Does he still carve?"

"He's dead."

"Sorry. What I meant is, did he carve again when he was retired?"

Mr. Thorpe shrugged. "I guess so. I remember he tried to get back to doing it daily, but his arthritis only let him work a few hours a week." He picked up the wooden rose again. "He did this in Florida. It took him a long time."

Stan thought of his own father. The old man had found his place in road work. And, he'd stuck to it. Everything...the monotonous work, asshole co-workers, mandatory overtime, the smoking to take the edge off. He didn't have a son with movie theaters to fall back on. And, he had a daughter who went to college instead of going to work.

The door to the den opened. The noise of the party grew louder. Mr. Thorpe looked up, and Stan turned around. Pete was leaning into the room. He smiled. "Hey, dad. Sorry to interrupt, but people are asking about when we're going to bring out the cake." He nodded to Stan.

"They can wait," Mr. Thorpe said.

Pete looked at Stan again briefly, and then closed the door.

"The theater business has been good to me," Mr. Thorpe announced. He took a longer drink of his brandy.

"Sounds like it," Stan said.

Mr. Thorpe opened a desk drawer absently and closed it. "June says that you work on an auto line."

He nodded. "In Novi. An engine assembly plant. But, I'm laid off right now." Isn't that what June had said? Going in the opposite direction, the small animal scurried by above him.

Mr. Thorpe looked up and tracked the rodent with his eyes. "Layoffs. That's the bad part of production work. There are no layoffs in the theater business. You might get a string of bad movies, but for the most part people still show up. Especially up here. They don't have much else to do."

"I imagine," Stan said.

Mr. Thorpe scratched his head. "June said, too, that you're not sure that you want to go back to work."

"Well, not on the line, anyway. I mean, I want to go back to work, but I'm not sure what kind of work."

Mr. Thorpe got up and walked back over to the liquor cabinet. "Auto line's good work. Good money. You can just walk away from that?" He poured himself another brandy.

Stan shook his head. "I don't like the work, really."

Mr. Thorpe turned around. He studied Stan for a moment. "A lot of people don't like their work."

"I know," Stan said. "But it's more than just not liking the work. I guess I'm just ready to get away from everything down there. Lots of memories, you know. You see, my wife and daughter—"

Mr. Thorpe's face loosened. He held up his hand. "June told me. I'm sorry. That's a damn sad story."

Stan nodded. "So I feel like I want to start over. This is a chance to think things through." He was surprised by how easily he could lie about the fictional layoff.

The tiny paws drummed by again above them. Stan imagined the rodent's zeal, all the crumbs and scraps of the party lying around.

Mr. Thorpe went back to the desk and sat down. "So, what are you going to do?"

The Question. "I'm not really sure, yet."

Mr. Thorpe studied him. "Not sure?"

"Well, I know I'm going to go back to work. I know that much. But, I don't really know what I want to do. It's been hard."

Mr. Thorpe was quiet for a moment. "You should go back to the line," he said. "Man's got to have a plan if he's going to leave his job. I mean, don't you think...I mean, aren't you a little worried?"

Stan felt his armpits heat up. "I guess I don't have a plan," he said. "But I don't think going back to the line is the right thing for me, either."

"Why not? It's as good a job as any...better than most. Good money. Good benefits. Hell, you have a house *and* a vacation place." Mr. Thorpe crossed his arms and leaned into his seat.

"I know, but they just don't mean much anymore. I just think I'd like to be doing something up here." The tiny pattering started across the ceiling again, but stopped abruptly.

"That's the dream, isn't it?" Mr. Thorpe said, glancing up. "Everyone south of Saginaw wants to move up here." He stared at a ceiling tile.

Stan thought of I-75 on a Friday afternoon. Bumper to bumper traffic. People trying to get to their cottages up North at fifteen miles an hour. Three-hour trips becoming five-hour trips. "You're right. Guys I worked with always talk about going up north like they're going to heaven. But I guess it's about more than just up North for me. I mean, the new location isn't the only reason I'd want to be up here."

"What do you mean?"

He swallowed. "Well, for one thing, there's June. I'd like to see if we can make something happen." He hoped he'd said it right.

Mr. Thorpe smiled and nodded his head. "Women. That's the one good reason that men make bad career choices." He took a sip of brandy. "I didn't tell you exactly why I started a movie theater in Gaylord. Hell, at eighteen I wanted to get as far from this town as possible. I always wanted to go to California. But, I met Kaye. She wanted to stay. So, I had to figure out a way to be rich right here."

Stan smiled.

"So, you really like June, huh?" he asked.

"We seem to get along pretty well."

The old man finished his brandy. He set the empty glass on the desk between he and Stan. "But, you don't know what you want to do up here?"

He shook his head. "I've been trying to figure that out."

"Like I said, there's not a lot of work up here. That's why people buy cottages, but *keep* their jobs down in the cities."

"I know," Stan said.

"But you'd like to stay up here?"

He nodded, wondering if the old man had Alzheimer's.

Mr. Thorpe reached for his brandy glass and slid it back and forth slightly on the desk. "I need a projectionist in Gaylord." He cleared his throat.

"Hmm?"

"One of my projectionists," Mr. Thorpe explained, "an older fella. He's moving to live with his sister in Texas. He'll be gone in two weeks. I need someone to replace him."

"Okay," Stan said. He was being offered a job. Something in his stomach simmered.

"Wouldn't take much to train you on the projectors. Couple of weeks."

A jolt ran through Stan. It was a feeling he used to get at the park when he'd look up from a magazine to check Shannon and she wasn't where he thought she'd be. When he'd find her, the relief would come. In Mr. Thorpe's den, no relief was coming.

"I could work it so that you're on maintenance some days. Mainly you come in and clean up the theaters and around the concession stand. Clean the bathrooms. It takes about two to three hours a morning. I could put together a forty hour week for you. Just to help you out."

Stan looked at Mr. Thorpe, but couldn't speak.

"It's not going to be line wages. But, it will be decent starting out money for up here. When we get you trained in, I can pay you seven fifty for running the projectors and six for cleanup. That's a little more than I pay most guys starting out."

Trying to guess what he could say, Stan lifted his drink to his lips. Finding emptiness, he set it down again. "I—"

Mr. Thorpe looked towards a corner of the ceiling. "Hold on," he said, putting his hand up. They sat quietly. Then a snap resounded mixed with a brief shrill squeak.

"Got him," Mr. Thorpe said proudly between his clenched, smiling teeth.

Old lion.

Stan pictured the mouse's broken-necked body clamped under the steel bow of the trap.

"Put the trap up there earlier this afternoon," the old man started. "But I never use cheese. I use graham cracker and peanut butter. They can't resist it. I was wondering when he'd get curious."

"I didn't know about the graham crackers."

Mr. Thorpe nodded. "I have another trick, too. Super glue. Super glue the cracker to the trigger. They yank like hell. Then, whack!"

They sat in silence for a moment.

"That's a problem with living in the woods. Lots of critters," Mr. Thorpe said.

Stan swallowed.

"You know, before you answer about the job, I wanted to let you know that this could lead to more. My manager over in Cadillac is getting close to retirement. A few years. If it worked out that way, maybe you'd take his position. I mean, nothing guaranteed, right? But, it's a possibility." He picked up his glass from the desk and went to the liquor cabinet again. "You need another?"

"No." He didn't need another job, either. Not yet.

Mr. Thorpe put the brandy bottle back in the cabinet and walked behind the desk. He sat and exhaled. "So, what do you think?"

Stan could feel his pulse at the surface of his skin. "I think it's a very generous offer. You don't even know me."

Mr. Thorpe shrugged benevolently. "June speaks highly of you. I like to help people out."

Stan smiled. She didn't really know him either. "How many screens does the theater have?" he asked.

"Two. Used to have one big screen, but we split it in the seventies to make two smaller theaters."

Stan nodded.

Mr. Thorpe smoothed a hand back and forth across the desk and then slapped his open palm against it. "So, what do you say to my offer? I need to go and blow out some candles." He smiled.

Stan scratched behind an ear. "Do I need to tell you right now?"

Mr. Thorpe's smile fell away. "Why *couldn't* you tell me now?"

"I don't know," he started, "I guess I'd like some time to think about it."

Mr. Thorpe sipped his brandy. He sucked his teeth. "What's to think about? You need a job up here, and I'm offering you a job up here."

He nodded. "I know. And I think it's a generous offer. I just want a little time before I say for sure whether or not I'm going to take it."

He studied Stan. "I don't really understand."

Stan's feet heated up in his shoes, his borrowed shoes. He cleared his throat. "I just don't know that I'm ready."

"Ready for what?" the old man asked impatiently. "Are you still considering keeping your job in Novi?"

"No," he said, but guessed that he just should have nodded his head.

"Then, what?"

"I'm not sure what I want. I'm not sure what I need."

"You don't know what? You don't know what you *need?*" Mr. Thorpe asked.

"It's not like it sounds. It's just—"

Leaning back into his chair, June's father shook his head. He filled his cheeks and exhaled. "I know what you've been through. And, I'm sorry. But, did June tell you what she's been through? Did she give you the details?" He pointed at Stan.

He thought about it and then shook his head.

Mr. Thorpe finished his brandy. "She didn't tell you what that sonuvabitch Vince put her through?"

Stan shook his head again. Vince, he thought. What was it about that name?

"Don't tell her I told you," Mr. Thorpe said. He looked at him.

"I won't." Stan hoped that it wouldn't be more than he wanted to know.

The old man cleared his throat. "She started to date Vince in high school. Went to senior prom with him. All that high school stuff. They kept dating after high school, too. Vince's dad owns a nice little nine-hole golf course outside of town. It's no premiere course, but they all make money up here. Vince worked for him. June took classes at the community college down in Grayling, enough business and accounting classes to do what she's doing now. When they hit twenty-five, Vince popped the question. Then they had their long engagement. About two years. Just this past May that engagement was supposed to turn into a marriage. But, three months before the wedding, Vince decided to call everything off. He packed up and moved to Colorado. Like that." Mr. Thorpe snapped his fingers.

"I didn't know," Stan confessed.

"Yeah," the old man nodded. "I guess *he* didn't know what he needed either."

The sarcasm wasn't lost on Stan, but he was working over more than just that. It wasn't so long ago that all of it had happened. And he never would have guessed that she was twenty-seven or twenty-eight. He'd always guessed that she was in her thirties. She seemed older, but now he knew that she was just weathered.

"That little asshole is already engaged to some new girl. Do you know what that did to June when she heard?"

Stan shook his head.

"Well, it was just embarrassing. Especially in a little town like this. I don't mean to come across as a hard ass," Mr. Thorpe said, "But the last thing she needs in her life right now is another Vince. So, when I hear you talking about not knowing what—"

A thought rushed into Stan's head. "Vince who?" he interrupted. "What's his last name?"

"Vince Sanderson," Mr. Thorpe said.

V.S.—the initials on the shirt he was wearing. Sure, it made sense that she might have some of Vince's clothes around, but why dress Stan up in them? He tried to fight the thought that she was simply trying to replace Vince with him.

"Stan."

Mr. Thorpe was looking at him over the desk. It felt like years ago when a teacher would catch him dozing in a marijuana daydream. "I'm listening," he said.

"I'm not saying anything," Mr. Thorpe said. "I'm waiting for you to say something."

He told him that he wasn't sure what to say. "What do you want to hear?"

"No bullshit. I want you to tell me that you're not out to hurt my daughter."

"I'm not," he said.

"I want you to tell me that you're being frank with her about everything." He tapped a finger on the desk.

"I am," he said. "She knows that I don't know exactly what I'm going to do. She's okay with it. She knows I need some time."

Mr. Thorpe looked into his face. "I've offered you a job. I want you to tell me that you're going to take it. It's money. You'll need money…while you're figuring things out. Just tell me that you're going to take it. It will make everything easier."

He thought about it. What was the harm? Why not take the job? He wasn't signing his life away. He'd just be agreeing to show a few movies and clean up popcorn. He'd still be able to think. But, his job on the line had looked like a good thing, too. After just a year working at the Novi plant, the job had him more than he had the job. And, it had happened quietly, but undeniably, like the slow encroachment of weeds. A point came when quitting just wasn't an option. "I can't. I can tell you that I'm going to think about it. I can tell you that much."

Mr. Thorpe looked at him and then stood up. "Well, people are waiting for me," he sighed. He came out from behind the desk and walked past Stan as though he were nothing more than an empty chair.

Stan pushed himself up and followed. Moving towards the door, he realized how hard he had made things. He thought to call out to Mr. Thorpe and tell him that he'd take his offer, but the old man had already opened the door and stepped out into the party. People were greeting him, ushering him away.

Stan got to the doorway. Gathered around Mr. Thorpe, a group of people led him towards a large dining room table. The cake on the table was on fire. Someone had taken the time to mark each year with a candle.

Thinking of the creek, he looked out the windows. It'd grown so dark that he couldn't even see the trees. Only the deck was visible in the intense glare of the floodlights. An arm slipped around him. June. She looked up at him, smiling. Her mouth was moving. Everyone was singing "Happy Birthday." He joined in for the last line or two. Then Mr. Thorpe blew out every candle with one breath, as if somebody had suggested that he couldn't.

Chapter XIX

Following June, Stan carried a plate with a piece of cake into one of the bedrooms. She left the lights off. Floodlight came in through the window, giving the room a faint glow, like the moon on a snowy night. They sat on the bed. A few light jackets were draped over the other side. Someone from the party laughed loudly. Setting her plate down, June put her arms around his neck and kissed him. It was a long kiss, like the start of something, but he felt nothing. Here in the half-light, was she imagining him as Vince? The jilting had been such a short time ago, and she had been with him so long she must still have feelings.

She pulled out of the kiss. "So, what did you and my dad talk about?" She took his hands into hers.

"He just asked me some questions, really." He had no proof, but she seemed different to him, scheming.

"What kinds of questions?"

Her tone was playful. "I guess you probably already know," he said.

"What do you mean?" she asked, the playfulness replaced by defensiveness.

"You must have known that he was going to offer me a job."

She shook her head while he spoke. "I didn't. I just told him about you and how you were out of work right now. I didn't ask him for anything." She let go of his hands.

She was telling the truth, something about the way she said it. He stood and walked over to the window. The deck was empty. The guests were probably still inside eating their cake. Bugs swarmed around the light. Something stuck in his throat, or in his chest, something heavy that he couldn't swallow or breathe away.

"Stan?"

He looked over at her. Holding her plate of cake again, she looked like a frightened little girl.

"What did you tell him?" she asked.

"Who?"

"My father. What did you tell him when he offered you the job?"

He turned toward the window again. Pete's son was on the deck, alone, holding his arms out, spinning himself in circles.

"I told him that I needed time to think about it," he said. Pete's son stopped, tried to walk, and then caught himself on a picnic table. He was laughing with nobody.

June was quiet. "What, *exactly,* do you need to think about?"

"I don't feel ready." He didn't turn towards her.

She stood and sighed. "Ready for what, Stan?"

"I don't want to rush into anything."

"Rush into what? He offered you a job at one of his theaters, right? I can't believe you said no."

She spoke quietly, but he could hear the welling of anger, too. He didn't have any response for her. "I didn't really say no," he whispered.

"Why don't you just take the job? Quit if you hate it. What else are you going to do? Is there some other job that you want?" she asked, raising her voice.

He shook his head.

"Then why can't you just take this job? He went out on a limb offering it to you. Now he probably feels stupid. I thought you wanted—"

Pete's son looked towards the house, his face attentive as though someone had called him. He ran out of sight. "I didn't say I wasn't going to take the job. I just told him that I wanted to think about it." He heard her sit on the bed again.

"How long do you think you'll think about it?"

"I'll probably let him know by Monday." Her fork clinked against her plate.

"Can you tell me *what* you're going to think about while you think about it?" she asked.

He turned towards her. "I know it sounds stupid. Believe me, I know. But when he asked me, something just didn't feel right. I just didn't think that I should answer too quickly."

She pushed at the cake. Then she pointed her fork at him. "You know, sometimes I think that you don't really have any idea what you're doing. You say or do something, but there's always some motive underneath it that you can't see."

He snickered. He couldn't help it.

"What?" she said. "I just think that you know what you really want, but you pretend that you don't. You're not being honest."

"I'm not being *honest?*" he said. He tried to keep from saying anything that might go too far. Over the years with Rachel he'd learned to think before speaking.

"No," she said, "I don't think you are. I think you're not taking the job because of me. Maybe you want nothing to do with me."

"I don't know why you'd think that," he said. "This isn't about you."

"What else am I supposed to think? Nothing else explains why you're acting this way." She set her plate on the floor, the cake only half-finished.

"The way I'm acting?"

She nodded. "It's more than just not accepting the job. It's the way you act around me. Earlier, on the deck, you seemed like you were acting jealous of Alan, and you were holding my hand. But now, even when we were just singing for my dad, you seemed distant. It was like it was hard for you to even have me around you."

He sighed and took a few steps towards her. "Look, I'm being honest. I like you. I want to see where things might go. But, I don't feel ready to say yes to any job that comes along. I know I shouldn't feel like this, but I do. Hell, I'll probably end up saying yes to your dad, but when he asked, I just didn't feel ready to commit."

She looked at him. "Do you honestly think that's why you're not taking the job? Or do you think it's something deeper?"

"That's what I think. Honestly. And what about you?"

"What do you mean?"

"I think both of us have some deeper things to work out," he said, cautiously.

She crossed her arms. "I don't know what you mean."

He walked closer. "Well, since we're trying to be honest, what about this shirt?" As soon as it came out, he wished he'd have phrased it differently.

She looked at the shirt. "What about it?"

"Come on," he said. "This is one of Vince's old shirts."

She looked at it again. "So what if it is?"

"You don't think it's a little odd?"

"In what way?"

"How can you ask that? I mean, you were with the guy for years, and then he broke off your engagement just a few months ago. And, then I come along and you dress me up in one of his shirts. Don't you think that you're trying hard to like me so we can pick up where you two left off? It just seems a little odd."

Her face changed. "That's a horrible thing to say. You show up at my door with *nothing* and I go…What was I supposed to give you to wear? One of my blouses? Or, did you just want to wear that stupid fishing sweatshirt?"

They'd been together for two days. She was acting like much more was on the line.

"How could you say something like that?" Her voice now was closer to tears.

The door to the room opened and June's brother started to walk in. He stopped. "Sorry, didn't know anybody was in here." He looked at Stan and then at June. "My jacket's in here. Dad asked me to pick up some more ice."

June bent for her plate again and picked at the cake.

"I'll go for ice," Stan said. He saw June's head snap up.

"What? No." Pete shook his head.

"No, really. Why should you leave your dad's party? I can run out and come back and nobody will even miss me."

Pete shrugged. "If you want. I probably shouldn't be driving, anyway."

"Good," Stan said. The idea of getting out by himself had him breathing easily again. June probably needed time to cool down. He patted the keys in his pocket.

She started to say something, but stopped.

He tried to look her in the face, but she was staring at the floor.

"I won't be long," he said. Pete turned towards the door. Stan followed him. He closed the door.

People looked to have finished their cake. Some were going back out onto the decks.

"Petey," Mr. Thorpe called. "Hurry back. Some folks want to see the old family movies. I need you to help me load the projector."

"I can do it *now*. Stan's going to get the ice."

Mr. Thorpe looked at Stan. Stan smiled at him, but the old man did not return the gesture. He turned to Pete. "All right, come on then."

Pete looked at Stan. "The guy owns six theaters, but he can't even run a goddamn projector anymore." He smiled.

"I'll see you in a little bit." Needling his way through the party, he made it to the front door. Since the sun had gone down, the night had cooled off, but he didn't care that he didn't have a jacket. He felt warm despite the cold.

Starting down the walk, he wondered if June even cared whether he came back or not. He knew he wasn't being fair to her. He'd need to apologize when he got back. The shirt. He'd gone too far. Why even bring it up? She'd been good to him, and he hated that he was always saying regrettable things to her. Still, she was coming on too strong.

He stopped in the middle of the long driveway. Ahead of him, the cars' silhouettes led down to the dark road. Across it, the stretch of blackness could have been a field or a lake. He knew it was a field, and yet he couldn't be sure. At its far end, it rose into the silhouetted trees. Down among the trunks, a small light burned. A window. Above it, stretched to infinity, the blue-black sky. It made him want to paint, something he'd never done. He couldn't be any worse than Van Gogh. He imagined the blacks and grays he'd use. The spot of yellow. The brush strokes. He had a name for the painting. 'Small Light in Darkness' Dizzy, he crouched down and leaned against one of the cars. Its cold seeped through Vince's shirt. The dizziness wasn't really bad. It felt more like the first drag on a cigarette at break time. It floored him for a moment.

He felt good, lifted. It had something to do with being away from everything. Mr. Thorpe. June's expectant face. Decisions. Here he could sit and think about nothing and breathe the night air. Night had been his favorite time at the cabin.

His sister came into his head. "Would you stop mooning over that cabin. You weren't happy there. You were hiding." Maybe she was right. And maybe this, the relief he was feeling, maybe it would turn to regret. "Of course you're going to regret this," his sister would say. "You're going to run away, and it will feel good for a little while, and then it will feel really bad. And when you run back, there won't be anything to run to." Though he hadn't seen her in some time, he pictured his sister's face. It was the kind of face that knew what it was talking about.

Then he thought of Chris, the kid from the gas station. Young. Pothead. But he knew enough to hold onto what is real.

Real. He imagined June where he'd left her on the bed among the coats. Maybe she was still there, staring into the darkness. Thinking. Maybe she didn't feel the smooth sleeve under her hand because she was more aware of something else. It had happened again. She'd let another man into her life. And, he too was an asshole.

A chill raced through him. He shivered it off.

Mr. Thorpe. Was he thinking about Stan at all? Or, had he written him off already? Sitting in the small theater in the dim glow of his family's past was he actually relieved that he wasn't stuck with such an oddball as his new projectionist? Would he tell June that he'd done what he could, but this new guy didn't seem very bright? Was the job offer no longer on the table? Maybe he would tell her to cut her losses.

Had he just lost her? Too much strange behavior on his part. The more he got distance from it, the more he realized the terrible thing he'd said about her giving him Vince's shirt. He looked again. Cars, a road, a field, trees, and sky. The small light was out. He didn't know anything about painting. He didn't know anything. He suddenly wanted to tell Mr. Thorpe that he would take the job. And, he wanted to see June.

He turned back towards the house. His heart seemed to beat in his throat. With a soft glow coming from almost every shaded window, it seemed otherworldly. He opened the door. The suddenness of the light hurt his eyes.

Chapter XX

Stan found the door that lead into Mr. Thorpe's home movie theater. He'd asked a guest, an older man, for directions. As he made his way through the party, he hadn't seen June. He was glad. When he saw her next, he wanted to have something to tell her.

The door closed behind him. In the darkness, he was only aware of the screen and the hazy cone of light projecting the picture. There was no sound. A little girl in a dress toddled around in what looked to be someone's backyard. Adult hands came into the picture now and again to help her up. As his eyes adjusted, he made out the silhouetted heads of the dozen or so people who were watching. He started down the aisle.

He looked in each row. Strange, half-lit faces turned and studied him. He soon saw who he guessed to be Mr. Thorpe sitting in an aisle seat. He crouched down next to him.

"Those are my hands," Mr. Thorpe whispered.

Stan nodded.

"It didn't take you very long to get ice," he said.

People turned to see who was talking. Then they turned back.

"I haven't gone yet. I want to talk to you first," he whispered. His heart thumped in his ears. Could everyone hear it?

Mr. Thorpe didn't turn toward him. "Look at my little girl," he said, watching the screen.

Stan looked. Little June was touching her hand to her mouth and then slinging the hand at the camera. She was beautiful. He thought of all the videos he had of Shannon. "Can I talk to you?" he whispered again.

Mr. Thorpe didn't say anything. He pushed himself up from the seat and walked up the incline towards the door. Stan followed. A few heads turned as they went by.

"What are we talking about?" Mr. Thorpe asked when the theater door closed behind them. They leaned against the wall.

"The job," Stan answered. "I want to take your offer. I'm sorry I didn't take it earlier."

Mr. Thorpe's mouth turned up slightly at the edges. "Can I ask how you made up your mind so quickly?"

"It's like you said, I need a job up here. Any job," he said. But that didn't sound right. "And this sounds better than just any job."

"And you'll be looking for other work, too?"

"I don't know. I don't really have any kind of work in mind."

"Because," Mr. Thorpe said, "it will take a few weeks to train you in on the projectors. I don't want to have you go through the training and then watch you grab up the first better offer that comes along."

Stan tried not to be angry with him for making this hard. "I can't say how long I'll stay, but I won't be applying anywhere else for a while."

Mr. Thorpe nodded. Then he held out his hand.

Stan took it, and they shook.

"Okay," Mr. Thorpe said. "You can start Monday." He put his palm against the theater door. "I'm glad you came around. June seems very fond of you."

Stan thanked him.

He found June out on the deck. She didn't see him right away, and he watched her talking with an older man. She was beautiful. Smiling, she talked and then she listened. Then, she noticed Stan. Within seconds she excused herself and went to him.

"What? Why are you smiling like that? You couldn't have gotten ice already."

He took her hand. "Come on," he said. He led her back to the bedroom where the coats were. Closing the door, he pulled her towards him and kissed her.

She kissed back for a moment and then pulled away. "What, Stan? Why are we here again?"

"I'm sorry," he said. "I'm sorry what I said about the shirt. That was out of line."

"It's all right."

"It's not all right. It was a shitty thing to say. I'm really sorry."

She leaned forward to kiss him again, but he caught her shoulders.

"I told your dad," he said.

"Told him?"

He smiled. "I told him I'd take the job. He said I can start on Monday."

"You did?" she asked. "You're sure that's what you want to do? I don't want you to feel forced—"

"I don't feel forced," he said. "It makes sense. It's what I should do. I want to." He pulled her up towards him, and they kissed again. Caught up, they fell against the door. The kissing insisted they go farther. He reached up under her shirt, found the smooth silk of her bra. Wanting more, he reached around behind her back.

She stopped his hands. "We can't in here...not in here."

He looked at her.

"Later," she said. "Tonight."

He smiled.

She looked at his pants and laughed. "You better wait before you go back out there."

He laughed.

Coming out of the room a few minutes behind her, he went for ice.

Chapter XXI

Stan stood on the porch looking out into the darkness. He felt better. He tried not to think himself out of the feeling. Sure he was moving pretty quickly with a girl he'd only just met but, considering the reclusive life he'd lived at the cabin, nothing seemed strange anymore. He patted his cigarettes. The door opened behind him. He turned. Petey.

"Hey," he said. "Dad just told me that you're going to be working for me." He smiled.

Stan grinned at the news, not having put it together earlier. Pete would be his boss. He liked Pete. "I'll be working for you?"

Pete nodded. "Yup."

Stan smiled. "Good," he said. "I wanted to talk to someone in management about a raise."

Pete laughed. "Hey, I said I was the manager. I didn't say I get to make any decisions."

Stan laughed, but he could tell there was some truth to what Pete had said. "Is your dad pretty free with his opinion about how you should run the place?" Stan had known foremen like that at the plant. They saw the utility man as a non-thinking extension of themselves. They used him as an extra set of feet for walk-throughs, eyes for spotting lazy workers, mouths for yelling. He had asked a utility man once how he could stand it. "How can I not?" he'd returned.

"Dad tells me what to do, and I do it. In a way it's not too bad. Makes the job easy. And, the old man's a perfectionist when it comes to work. He blames himself for every mistake. He never calls me on the carpet for anything." He looked into the darkness at something. He coughed.

"Doesn't sound all bad," Stan said. Didn't really sound all good, either.

"My job? Hell no, it's not bad. I'm almost completely unnecessary, but I get paid pretty well for it." He laughed.

Stan forced a laugh himself. Then they both looked off towards the driveway. A car went by.

Pete cleared his throat. "Take a walk with me," he said, stepping out of the porch light and disappearing into the darkness.

Stan looked after him, but didn't move right away.

"Come on," he called.

Stepping out of the light, he could make out Pete's gray silhouette. He followed it around the corner of the house. Pete leaned up against the siding. Around the next corner, voices from the deck talked loudly. "Hold on," he said, talking like he was chewing a blade of grass. He struck a match, and his face glowed in its fiery light. He shook out the flame. Tight-lipped, he sucked in.

A joint.

Pete handed it to Stan, its small cherry glowing dimly. How many times had he passed a joint back and forth back in his high school days? Too many times to count. He brought it to his mouth and took a quick hit. Boss might not always be right, but he's still the boss, he joked to himself. He handed the joint back to Pete.

"No," he said. "Take a real hit. It's good stuff."

Stan took a long drag. Smiling at Pete, he held it for as long as he could. His head filled with something like cotton candy. "Wow."

Pete took another long hit. He held it and then talked the smoke out. "It's prime weed," he said. "Comes on strong, but you come down long." He smiled and handed the joint back.

Stan took another quick hit. His cheeks seemed to loosen and droop down on his face. "Man," he said. "That is good. Too good. It's been a long time for me. I think I've had enough already." He passed it back.

Pete smiled. "All right," he said. He took another long drag.

The darkness of the trees loomed above them. Stan hadn't realized that the woods were so close on this side of the house. Light shined from the deck. Someone's elbow poked out over the railing. He studied it. Something about it seemed important, tender even. He smiled at the elbow.

Pete asked if he didn't want one more hit.

"No," he said. He opened his mouth a few times, but couldn't lose the tingly feeling in his cheeks. He laughed. "I'm real good."

Pete nodded. "One of my projectionists gets this stuff for me. He's got a cousin in Flint."

Light-headed, Stan crouched down against the side of the house. Pete joined him. He wasn't sure how much time had passed, but after a while he no longer heard Pete hitting the joint. The elbow was gone when he looked for it. Surfacing from the muck that the pot had made of his mind, he had a thought. "So, it doesn't bother you at all?" he asked.

"What?" The word seemed to float from Pete's mouth and then pop into sound, as though a child had blown it from a plastic bubble stick.

"Working for your old man."

He was quiet for a moment. "Not really. It's not all that bad. It's pretty easy, you know?" He moved his fingers in the dirt between them.

"I don't mean if it's hard or not. I just mean that you don't mind that— Well, you just think it's what you want to do."

"What I want to do?" Pete asked.

"Yeah," he said. Some of the fog from the pot lifted, or maybe it was the weed bringing out his questions. "What would you be doing if your old man didn't own a theater?"

Pete lifted a handful of dirt and let it run out the bottom of his fist like sand in an egg timer. "I don't know. Who cares, right? My old man *does* own a theater. Theaters. When he dies, I'm going to own theaters. June, too, I guess. Not too bad for you if you stick around," he offered good-naturedly.

"I guess," Stan said. He'd never really thought about what June stood to inherit. "But didn't you ever want to do anything else?"

Pete shook his head. "I've been in a theater all my life. At ten years old, dad already had me cleaning up after Saturday matinees. By fifteen I was an usher. It's pretty much in my blood, I guess. I can't really imagine doing anything else."

"Are you happy?"

"Happy?"

The shish of footsteps came across the front yard.

"Oh shit, get up," Pete said.

They both stood. A silhouette appeared at the corner of the house. "Petey?" Mr. Thorpe asked. "Is that you?"

"Yeah, Dad."

Mr. Thorpe took a few steps closer. "Who's that with you?"

"It's me," Stan said, when Pete didn't answer.

Mr. Thorpe studied them for a few seconds. "What are you doing out here?"

Again, Pete didn't say anything. It didn't strike Stan that he was going to. He cleared his throat. "Pete was telling me about the job," he started, finding the lie as its details came into his head. "He was telling me about the projectors and the work schedule. We were on the porch, but the bugs were too much in the light. We were just kind of walking around the yard. Taking a little walk, I guess."

Mr. Thorpe looked at them. "I need you to load another film. They want to see that old Christmas footage."

Pete nodded and then smiled at Stan. "I'll talk to you when you get back."

Mr. Thorpe looked at Stan. "You haven't gone for ice yet?" he asked. "I figured you were just getting back."

"I talked with June for a little bit," he explained. "I'm leaving right now."

Mr. Thorpe turned around, shaking his great lion head, and Pete followed him. They left Stan on the side of the house.

Chapter XXII

Stan turned at the end of the driveway and started towards the car. Away from the lights of the house, he felt uneasy in the thick darkness. He tried to shake it off. He could still feel June's breasts in his hands, and he imagined what later would be like. Then he'd had a joint, and that was good, too. Something was coming together.

He reached into his front pocket, found his cigarettes, and pulled one out that wasn't broken. No light. He shrugged. There'd be a cigarette lighter in the car.

Up ahead, near where he guessed they'd parked, he saw the glowing orange tips of others smoking. He put his cigarette in his mouth and walked towards them. His feet crunched in the gravel of the shoulder. "Can I get a light from one of you guys?" he asked. He could make out at least four silhouettes.

They turned towards him. "Holy shit, look who it fucking is." It was Alan Marsh's voice.

Stan stopped. His spine burned with the fiery warning chemicals that were telling him to run. Two of the silhouettes were sitting on the hood of June's car. They hopped down to standing.

"I can't believe it," Alan snickered. "I can't fucking believe it."

His voice sounded clearer, steadier, as though he'd sobered some since he'd last talked to Stan. The other silhouettes moved closer. "You got shitty luck, pal" one said.

"This is the asshole I was telling you guys about," Alan said. "He said I was a piece of shit."

"I didn't say that," Stan said. Anything might happen, and he moved so a car was to his back. Couldn't let someone get directly behind him. The other men positioned themselves so he was trapped against the car. He counted. There were four, plus Alan, who stood right in front of him. His pulse raced in his temples. He clenched his fists.

"You said something about shit, didn't you?" Alan asked, sneeringly.

"I said…" he started, but then he stopped. Alan was baiting him.

"You said what? Oh, I remember now. You said I wasn't going to *do* shit." He pointed a finger in the air.

Stan didn't say anything. A car came down the street. Its headlight flashed the group of men into stark relief. For a moment, in the light, they were frozen. None of them looked hesitant. The car kept going.

"Do you think this is going to do anything?" Stan asked. He cleared his throat. "Do you think June's going to—"

Alan planted his hands into his chest and shoved him against the car. "Don't even fucking say her name. Who the fuck are you to be saying her name?"

Stan came off of the car fast and drove his fist into Alan's nose. He wanted to nail at least one other guy, but they moved quickly and had his arms pinned before he could do anything else. A knee landed in his groin. His vision went black.

Trying to ease the furnace of pain, he squeezed his thighs against his testicles. He'd have been on the ground, but the men were holding him up. After a few seconds, he vomited. "You fucking pig," a voice said. For a while the pain came in steady waves, and an uncomfortable sensation tingled in his stomach. "You all right, Alan?" someone asked. Alan didn't answer. Time passed. Then Stan became aware of a noise. His pain kept him from discerning it. Then the noise became distinct, someone kicking gravel. He lifted his head.

Slightly bent, holding his nose, Alan walked back and forth on the shoulder of the road. "Goddabbit," he hissed, and kicked the gravel again. Stan tasted the dustiness in the air. A moment later, Alan walked over and grabbed his hair. "You bwoke my fuckig node," he said. His fist came down and knocked Stan's face toward the ground.

Black. Then a little light. The men pulled him up, their hands like vices, and rested his back against the cold car. His cheek throbbed like a heart. Blood filled his mouth. He spit.

Alan telegraphed a punch, a punch Stan could have easily blocked had his arms been free. The fist landed in his stomach. The pain took a moment to register. When it came, he coughed up more vomit. He spit it and more blood. The men set him against the car again. "Maybe he's had enough," one of the men said.

Alan grabbed Stan's ponytail. "You fuckig dwop her," he shouted. "You fuckig dumbp her and get out. You got it?"

Stan looked at him. "Why not just you and me?" he mumbled. "Even now. Just tell these guys to let go. And then just you and me. One on one."

Alan jabbed him in the nose. Pain imploded and he couldn't see. He tried to block it out, tried to look ahead. This couldn't go on much longer. It hurt to punch someone. He'd have to let up soon.

"You better stop now," a voice Stan hadn't heard before said. "He's got the point."

"I just watt him to say it's ova. Just say it's ova," Alan said. "Just say you're dud wid her." He wasn't yelling.

"All right," he tried to shout, but it came out weakly. "It's over."

It was quiet for a time. He tried to look up, but couldn't. The hands let him go suddenly, and he dropped on the ground. He grabbed his groin and rolled on his side.

"It fuckig better be ova," Alan said.

Stan tried to nod. He'd gotten them to stop. That's what he wanted. The next time he saw Alan things would be different.

"Did you fuckig hear me?" Alan shouted.

A foot landed in Stan's lower back. The pain was too much. He writhed. Someone may as well have been operating on his kidneys without anesthetics.

When he was aware again of things like sound, he heard nothing. No feet in the gravel, no whispers. They were gone. His nose, his crotch, his stomach, his back…everything competed to throb with the most pain. In the distance, a car near June's father's house started up. It spit up gravel. In a moment, he saw a flash of light through his eyelids, and then blackness again. Silence.

Lying still, he started to shiver. He wasn't certain how much time passed, but eventually he was able to sit up and rest his back against the car. Something moved in the grass beyond the shoulder. He could hear the party. The pain in his groin and stomach had dulled, but his kidney and nose still throbbed. He pulled out his cigarettes. He couldn't find one that wasn't busted. He felt like he might be able to stand.

Had an hour passed since the last kick? He wasn't sure. When he put weight on his feet, the pain came back to his groin. He was able to stand through it. He touched his nose and guessed that it probably wasn't broken. He imagined catching Alan sometime maybe coming out of the theater late at night. He'd get him by himself and return the favor.

He lowered his back gently against the driver's seat. He found a position and rested for a few minutes. He started the car and turned the heat up. It blasted him with cold air, but he left it on and waited for it to warm. He sat for a long time.

He tried to imagine working at the movie theater. Maybe it wouldn't be so bad. It certainly would be different from the plant. He guessed that after the movie started, the projectionist had a lot of time by himself. He had learned to enjoy that. He could use the time to think, though he wasn't sure if thinking had gotten him anywhere. Mainly he'd thought himself into this trouble, frustration.

But what would the job be, really? Night after night of the same movie, the same characters, same dialogue, same outcome. He'd eat the same popcorn, and in the morning he would clean up the popcorn that others had spilled. It's the kind of work that brings a paycheck. He'd had that already. But what if, like Mr. Thorpe suggested, it turned into a management position? Could that be more challenging? Or, would it too have its routine? Hiring concession people, ordering stock, doing payroll—none of it sounded very interesting. And, if things worked out, he might marry June. Some day, partnered with Pete, they'd own all six theaters. What kind of money would that mean?

The vents eventually blew lukewarm air, and he warmed in it. For now he would get ice. He'd wrap some in a paper towel and hold it to his nose. The idea of it helped him shift into drive and pull away.

He didn't know where he was going. Mr. Thorpe's road eventually ended at a stop sign. He could turn left, right, or drive straight ahead into the woods. Left looked as good as anything. It wouldn't be long before he'd come to a gas station. They'd have ice. Then he could go back. What would he tell June? Tilting the rearview mirror he examined his face. In the dim light from the dashboard, he couldn't tell much, but his nose looked different. It was bigger, swollen. In shadow, his entire face looked grotesque.

The road didn't change. Blacktop and trees. He guessed he'd already gone five miles. Nothing lay ahead of him except darkness. He looked for any kind of light, but saw only what he guessed were the glowing eyes of animals.

He drove a few more miles. A spot of light shone back in the woods. He slowed down and passed a mailbox that had been fitted with wings and a propeller so as to resemble an airplane. It struck him that he knew the mailbox from someplace. Then it hit him. He was on the same road Dale had used to come into Gaylord. He imagined the turns that had taken them from the cabin to this road. He could find Dale's place. He wanted to. He could clean up. He could find out about Dale's ear. He drove faster, no longer looking for light. He passed a gas station. It was open, but he didn't care. He thought of cigarettes, slowed, but then changed his mind and punched the gas again. He'd left Mr. Thorpe's place without money. He shook his head.

On the drive in, Dale had really opened up to him, had tried to help him. Maybe now he could set him straight. About the job, Mr. Thorpe, June. All of it. He wasn't sure if he'd done the right thing. He'd lost something that he couldn't get back. It wasn't Rachel or Shannon or the house. It was something without a name. He mourned it. Was he being a fool?

He guessed what Dale would say.

"You did what you have to do. You've got your whole life to figure out the other things. But in the meantime you've got someone to help you work it out. What other choice is there? Being alone?" It's what he imagined Dale would say, but he needed to hear it.

Chapter XXIII

His headlights soon illuminated the front entrance to Dale's place. Dale's car was there. Dim light glowed from within the cabin. Maybe he was already asleep.

The shotgun. He didn't want to startle Dale. He leaned back into the seat, and his kidney throbbed with pain. He shifted and found a more bearable position. He watched the cabin. He was parked on a rise slightly above it, and he looked down on it where it glowed warmly in the surrounding darkness. His position reminded him of a painting he'd seen in two different hunting camps. It was a night scene. In the foreground, a wolf lay on a ridge looking down on a snowbound cabin. Pale light glows from the windows and casts long rectangles on the snow. White wisps of smoke rise into the blue darkness that dominates most of the scene. For a time he'd looked for the painting to hang in his own cabin. Something about it had stayed with him. It looked like a wolf. It looked like a cabin. That was art.

Nothing changed in Dale's cabin. He'd have to try the front door. He wasn't sure how long it had been since he'd left Mr. Thorpe's place. He opened his door and stepped out. The night seemed warmer, and he wondered if the river could have something to do with it. He'd heard that towns near the Great Lakes were a little warmer in early winter. Something to do with water. He'd never learned the details of why. He closed his door.

"Dale?" a voice called from the blackness, "Is that you?"

He turned towards the voice, but saw nothing. Branches snapped under the other person's tread. Then the noise stopped.

"You just getting in, Dale?" the man asked.

Stan guessed by the man's voice that he was older, maybe Dale's age. "It's not Dale," he called. "I'm...I'm a friend of his."

The other man didn't say anything. His footsteps started again and grew gradually louder. His silhouette faded in through the darkness. "You're a friend of Dale's?"

"Yeah," he said. "Actually, I have a cabin upstream. I met Dale not too long ago. I'm just stopping by."

"I just got up myself," the other man said, "from Detroit. I usually come over and have a beer with Dale. My name's Wes Johnson." He extended his hand. His gray hair almost seemed to glow.

Stan shook his hand and told Wes his name.

"Where you from?" Wes asked cordially.

"Novi."

The older man nodded. "Got a nephew in Novi," he said. He looked towards Dale's cabin. "Well, let's go wake him up."

"You think he's asleep?"

"He's always napping, but I don't think he's in bed, yet."

"I don't know," Stan said, "maybe I should just take off. It's getting late."

"Just come on," Wes said. "He'd be happy to see you."

He shrugged.

The two men walked down the slope towards the cabin. A nearby animal scurried off into the woods. Through the windows, several lamps glowed. Wes rapped on the front door, and they waited.

"I-75 was a bitch tonight," he said. "Took me five and a half hours to get up here from the city. When did you drive up?"

"Actually," he said, "I've been up for a few weeks." He touched his nose and winced. Tender, but not broken.

"Lucky," Wes said. He rapped on the door again. "Come on," he shouted. "Guy could die of thirst out here." He smiled at Stan.

A moment later, he stepped over to the kitchen window that looked in on the cabin. "Sure enough," he said. "Asleep in his chair." He rapped his knuckles against the glass. "Dale!"

Stan stepped over to the window. The top of Dale's head poked up over a recliner. He faced away from the window towards the fireplace, where a bed of embers still glowed softly. "Maybe we should let him sleep," Stan said.

Wes rapped on the glass again, rattling the pane. "Guy's going deaf," he said. He walked back to the front door and turned the knob. The latch clicked free of the strike plate. "Well," Wes said, opening the door, "If we're quiet enough, we can have a beer and we won't have to hear one of his boring stories." He stepped in the cabin. "Right, Dale?" he shouted.

Stan followed him. Did Dale stir? Maybe they should leave him alone. The smell of the smoldering fire was good. It smelled like his own cabin. He enjoyed it for a moment, and then closed the door.

Wes walked over to the refrigerator. "You're kidding me," he said, crouching down. He moved some things around. Bottles knocked against bottles. "He's out of beer. Well, we'll wake him up and then head over to my place. I've got a little brew."

Despite the warm cabin, Stan went cold. He'd come to talk to Dale privately. He also needed to get ice and get back to Mr. Thorpe's party. And, get back to June. He imagined going over to Wes's place where he wouldn't be able to say anything to Dale, at least not anything he wanted to say. "You know, maybe I'm just going to head out," he said.

"No, we can wake him up," Wes said. He rose up out of the refrigerator and closed the door. "Holy shit!" he said, taking in Stan's face. "What happened?"

"What? Oh," he said, thinking quickly. "I had a little fall coming down the back steps of my place. It was weird. Just, boom, right down on my face."

Wes studied him.

"I thought Dale might have aspirin," Stan said. "My head's pounding."

Wes nodded. "Looks like it hurts."

"It does," Stan confirmed. He wanted to leave.

Wes walked over to Dale and shook him. "Get up, lazy." He pulled his hand back. "Dale?" he murmured. "Oh no, Dale."

"What?" he asked, but he knew before Wes even nodded.

"Dead."

Wes walked backwards until his heels hit the couch. He sat down.

Something in the fireplace popped. After a moment, Stan walked around the chair so he could see Dale's face. He sat as though sleeping, head tilted towards his right shoulder. His ear was bandaged. When they welled up, the tears surprised Stan. He'd found his father the same way. Dead in a Lay-Z-Boy.

"He must have died sometime after he threw a few logs on the fire. Heart attack, maybe," Wes mumbled.

"Maybe," Stan said. He sniffed.

"Were you guys close?"

"I guess so," he said. "It's hitting me harder than I thought something like this would." He moved and then sat on the stone hearth of the fireplace. The embers still threw a faint heat. They sat for some time looking at Dale, not talking. The smoldering coals crackled softly.

"I didn't know him, really" Wes started, talking low. "I mean, we've had a lot of beers together, but I don't really know much about him. I know he's got a kid, maybe two. Mainly we just shot the breeze when we talked. Redwings. Tigers." He sniffed. "Probably should try to get in touch with the kid." He rubbed his chin.

Stan looked at Wes. "How long have you known him?"

"Ten years or so. Mainly we just saw each other in the summers."

Stan nodded. "When we talked, he mentioned *kids* so I guess it's more than one. Maybe there's a number for one of them somewhere in the cabin." He thought about the talk he'd had with Dale on the way in to Gaylord. He knew more about the man than Wes did.

"I'd guess," Wes said, nodding.

Stan looked at Dale again. The tears didn't come. He'd been crying for his own father as much as anything. He walked into the kitchen and started to open drawers.

"Looks like it happened in his sleep," Wes said.

"Yeah, that's exactly what happened to my dad."

"That's a blessing, I guess," Wes said.

That's what the doctor had told Stan's family. His father's death in his sleep had been a blessing. He had allowed himself to see it that way at the time because it brought some kind of comfort. But it didn't seem like a blessing. The guy put thirty-three years in on the Wayne County Road Works. Thirty-three years that probably didn't look very different from each other. Then, he spent another six months getting used to retirement. When he finally had it down, at least somewhat, when he finally felt like maybe he could do something he wanted to do, a fly fishing trip to Montana, a massive coronary wiped him out in his sleep.

In a drawer below the telephone he found a book of phone numbers. "There are some names and numbers here," he said. "Did he ever mention his kids' names?"

Wes nibbled his lip and looked up toward the ceiling. "Not that I can remember," he said. "He may have, but it didn't stick with me." He stood and walked over to the chair.

A number next to the names Cindy and David stood out for him. "Cindy or David ring a bell?" Stan asked.

Wes pulled an afghan over Dale's head. "No," he said. "Not really. Maybe. I don't know."

"Well, I'm going to try this number. Maybe someone on the other end will at least know the name of one of his kids."

Wes nodded. "You know," he said, "I think I'll run over to my cabin and call the police. They'll need to get the coroner out here."

"Makes sense," he said. He started to dial the number, but then stopped. "Hey," he said, catching Wes with his hand on the doorknob, "do you at least know Dale's last name?"

"Fletcher."

Stan finished dialing the number. Listening to the ringing, he had no idea what he would say. Three rings. Four rings. What if an answering machine picked up?

Someone finally answered. A man's voice.

"Could I speak to David or Cindy?"

The man on the other end sighed slightly. "This is Dave."

"Okay," Stan said, searching for where to begin. "I'm calling…I'm calling from—"

"Look," Dave started, sounding exasperated, "I'm supposed to be on some kind of No Call list. We really don't take—"

"No," he said. "I'm not a telemarketer. I'm calling from Dale Fletcher's cabin."

The other end was quiet.

"Do you know Dale?" Stan asked.

"He's my wife's father. My father-in-law. Who is this?"

Something in the fireplace popped again. "My name is Stan Carter. I have a cabin on the same river as Dale. I stopped by tonight to see him, and I found him in his chair."

"Found him?"

He swallowed. He was somewhat relieved to be speaking to the son-in-law instead of the daughter. "He passed away."

"He's dead?"

"It looks like it happened in his sleep," he said, trying to be comforting. He didn't call it a blessing.

"Oh God," Dave said after a moment. "This is going to hit her hard."

"I'm sorry," Stan said. "Another guy was here too, a guy named Wes Johnson. I think he's a friend of Dale's."

"I don't know the name."

"Well, he's gone to call the police. I'll give them your number when they get here. I'm sure they'll want to talk to you." He tried to look out the sliding glass door, but it only reflected the room and his own image back to him.

"Sure," Dave said.

Stan didn't know what more to say.

"We were going to meet him up there in a few weeks," Dave said hollowly. "It'd been a long time. And now...this is going to kill her."

Chapter XXIV

Stan sat on the couch. The call was over. The son-in-law. He felt lucky. Unmoving as he was under the afghan, Dale could have been a grandfather playing hide-and-seek. The grand-children would never find him again. He wondered how long Dave had meant when he said it'd been a "long time" since they'd seen him. He knew the regrets Cindy was about to feel. He felt them with his own father. For months he'd worked the same questions over in his head: Why didn't I try to talk to him more? Why couldn't I have been a better son? Why didn't I ever learn to fly fish like he wanted me to? Why didn't I know him better?

A clock on the wall read eleven thirty. He remembered that it was a half an hour fast. Still, June was probably worried. Maybe she'd even cried. He didn't want to think about what Mr. Thorpe was thinking. He considered leaving, but knew that he should stay for the police. He took another look at Dale and then walked out onto the back of the property. He slid the door closed. The river murmured to him.

It moved in a slip of black against the gray around it. Brief strings of white flashed across the surface. The Black. He sighed, glad to be away from the body and everything else he had to think about. He lay back on the grass.

Overhead, the starry sky flickered. He leaned against his elbows. In the cabin, Dale sat under the afghan. Would it strike Cindy, maybe at the funeral as someone spun a half-true eulogy, that she didn't really know her father at all? Not as a man with desires of his own.

Stan turned back towards the river. It was all around him. In his ears. In his nose. He could almost taste it. Feel it. A fish, a big brown he guessed, gulped something off the surface. A story he'd heard from someone or seen in a movie drifted into his head. When more of the details came to him, he remembered that it was a short story that he'd been assigned to read in high school. He hadn't read it, but he remembered the teacher explaining the ending.

He'd paid attention because there'd been something odd about a mother washing her dead son's body with her daughter-in-law. The man was a miner, and his coal-smeared surface needed to be cleaned before the funeral. Bringing the detail out, making it explicit by talking about it, the teacher had gotten everyone to be quiet, even those in the back who hadn't read.

"And then after," the teacher had said, nearly shouting, "what did she see? There he was stretched out naked, dead, and clean in the living room. What did the wife see?"

Nobody in the back dove for the obvious jokes, and even the students in the front rows kept their hands down.

The teacher read a few lines from the story. He'd used them as evidence to suggest that the character had a moment of awakening. She'd seen something she hadn't seen before. The man lying in front of her—the man she'd slept with, had children with, fought with—was a complete stranger to her. And, when he'd been alive, she was a stranger to him. "Death," the teacher said, "had shown her what she really had needed to know while the man was alive."

Stan saw himself in the story as both the miner and the miner's wife. A part of him lay stretched out in front of him, and another part studied the prone part, and neither part knew the other. He lay his head back on the grass.

The stars were still there. Above him the grayness was broken now and again by tiny flickers of black. He closed his eyes and imagined himself as a bat skimming the surface of the river, bouncing sound off insects, opening his jaw. He felt one go in and flutter briefly against the inside of his cheek. Blood exploded in his mouth as he bit down. Then sound again. Location. Eating.

Pain radiated from his kidney, jarring him from near-sleep. Minutes passed, and it felt as though the pain were something else, an instinct that he kept from the surface, but then it emerged. He sat up. The river was the same. The stars were above him. The moon. The night had grown no cooler than it had been, but something made him edgy. His breathing shallowed, and his chest felt constricted. He went back into the cabin.

The operator said there were two listings for Peter Thorpe in the Gaylord area.

Mr. and Petey. "Can you tell me the street addresses?"

She did. One lived on Jefferson Avenue and the other on a county road. He took the number for the county road.

The phone rang. A small flame leapt up from a black log. Its light flickered in the room. Small tufts of Dale's hair poked up through the knit of the afghan.

Mr. Thorpe picked up. The noise of the party came through in the background.

"It's Stan."

"Did you go to Detroit for ice?"

"Not exactly," he said.

The other end of the line was quiet for a moment. "Is everything okay?"

"I'm okay. The car's okay." His forehead tingled with heat.

"Do you want to talk to June?"

Stan cleared his throat. "I called to talk to you."

"We can talk when you get back. I've got a party going on here. Old friends just—"

"I can't take the job."

Silence.

"It's not that I don't appreciate the offer," he continued. "I do. It just doesn't feel right."

"Feel right?"

Stan switched hands and wiped his palm on his pants. "I can't explain it."

"You're a piece of work," Mr. Thorpe said. "Look, stay away from June. Do her that favor, would you?"

The phone beeped and the connection went dead. He felt the thud of his racing heart.

He went outside again. Slashes of moonlight flashed from the river. He breathed deeply. A moment later, the light coming through the sliding glass door behind him shifted. He turned. Wes was coming through the front door. A police officer was with him.

Stan bolted and camouflaged himself in the darkness near the river. He watched inside the cabin. Wes and the officer turned down the afghan and looked at Dale. The officer, dressed in the stark blue uniform, looked at the body, nodded, and then pulled the afghan up again.

The process that Wes had started with his phone call might yet take a couple of hours. The police would have questions. The coroner would have questions. None of it would be important, just the routine that follows any death. Stan didn't want to talk or think. His cabin was only a half mile or so upstream. He could smell it.

He left Vince's clothes on the lawn. The river was his only choice. Throwing it next to the jeans, he was glad to be rid of the heaviness of the shirt. He kept the band t-shirt on. It was long enough that it covered him.

The water was cold until his feet numbed. It wasn't deep. Even in the middle, it barely came above his knees. The Black was a shallow river in many places. He could make good time even walking upstream. It would take him an hour. Maybe less. He scooped handfuls of water and splashed them against his sore face, cooling the pain.

Little white specks glinted in the river like shooting stars. Bending closer, he saw that it was a spinner fall of the ephorons he'd seen hatching only two days before. The adults had emerged, mated, and now were dead.

As he moved against the current, the water climbed higher on him—thighs then waist then chest—and the current grew stronger. The tag alder was thick at the edges. He would have to try to swim it.

Launching himself forward, he worked hard against the surface. He stroked until his shoulders and hips went numb with exhaustion. He tried to stand but found nothing. The current pushed him downstream to the far side of the hole again.

He stood in the shallows with his hands on his knees, sucking wind. He stared ahead into the moon-streaked river moving past him.

"He's clearly not very stable," Mr. Thorpe would say to June.

"Haven't you had enough shenanigans from Vince?"

"Dude, are you nuts?" Chris would ask, taking a minute to hit his joint.

"Stan, what did I tell you," his sister would say. "I said not to do anything stupid. You had a chance to be happy, and you threw it away."

If Dale were alive, he'd say the same thing. "Don't throw the girl away," he'd say. "What else do you have?"

Stan shivered. The heat he'd built up from swimming was gone. His breathing was normal again. Still, he felt something he could have. Not June. It was something else, something bigger. Something in the trees' silhouettes black around him. Something in the sky stretched gray and starry above. Something in the river's churning song. He wanted to dissolve into all of it—and come back as something else.

The t-shirt hung heavily on him soaked with cold. He pulled it over his head and threw it into the tag alder. He dove headlong into the hole again. He swam deep. The water was all around him, but slower in its depths. Closing his eyes, he imagined steelhead trout returning in the spring. He felt his own strong fins. The water pushed and pushed and pushed. He swam against its insistence. His body was made for rivers. He would swim past this hole. He could make it.

Jeff Vande Zande lives in Bay City, Michigan, with his wife and their two children. He teaches English at Delta College and enjoys fishing Michigan's many trout streams. His short fiction has appeared in *Passages North, Night Train, The MacGuffin, Crab Creek Review,* and *Iron Horse Literary Review,* among others. His two books of fiction include *Emergency Stopping and Other Stories* (Bottom Dog Press) and *The Bridge* (March Street Press), a small collection of stories that take place around the Mackinac Bridge, and *Transient* and *Tornado Warning* (March Street Press), two collections of poetry. He maintains a website at http://www.jeffvandezande.com